"Travis Richardson proves, yet again, that his name belongs at the top of the list of master short storytellers. *Bloodshot and Bruised* collects prose both sharp and serrated, then gives rise to a voice that is bleak, uncompromising, and funny. You won't be able to put it down."

—Eryk Pruitt, author of *What We Reckon* and
The Long Dance podcast

"Steeped in blood and grit, *Bloodshot and Bruised* is taut, twisted, and thrilling. Travis Richardson has an exceptional talent for bringing shady characters to life in all of their vengeful, double-crossing glory. His stories represent the dark side of the American Dream, and they are unforgettable."

—Hilary Davidson, Anthony Award-winning
author of *One Small Sacrifice*

"Travis Richardson brings us a collection of two-fisted tales—one fist stained with meth and tobacco juice, the other one with dabs of avocado and blood—in this outstanding collection of funny, dark and thrilling crime stories from both the West Coast and the South."

—Jordan Harper, author of Edgar Award-winning
She Rides Shotgun

BLOODSHOT AND BRUISED

Travis Richardson

The characters and events in this book are fictitious. Any similarity to real persons, living or dead, is coincidental and not intended by the author.

Cover design by WordSugar Designs
Interior design by Teresa Wong

ISBN: 9781728888231

To Sarah and Stephen, who have critiqued every story in here and several dozens more.

Table of Contents

BLOODSHOT:
TALES FROM THE SOUTH

The Day We Shot Jesus on Main Street

IF THERE ARE two things you oughta know about Lynchwood, it's that nobody votes Democrat and nobody blasphemes the Lord God Almighty . . . at least in public. Now Chad Parrish would've broken rule number one had he lived long enough, and it's because of rule number two he didn't ever register.

He was always makin' a ruckus about things that we weren't gonna change. Like changin' our minds about them gays or interracial marriages. See, Chad was born in the wrong place. Had he been raised in New York, he might've been praised by liberal comrades for bein' a creative bastard and an all-around troublemaker. But here in Lynchwood, that bird don't fly.

Chad had gathered some of the town's ne'er-do-wells— you know, them boys who don't play football and complain about the school's arts program not getting enough funding. Yep, them types. It seems that Chad had a bug up his butt about the Lynchwood Ministry and how we were so successful. It's a congregation the media might label a megachurch, but it's practically the only house of worship all of us in Lynchwood go to, 'cept for Chad and a handful of other sinners.

Well, we're all passin' the collection plates during Sunday services when five of these fellows, dressed in robes and wearing fake beards and long-haired wigs, come burstin' through the doors shoutin' like banshees. They grabbed the collection money and ran straight for the pulpit. Then they threw them plates of cash and coins on the ground and started shoutin' somethin' about the scripture of John and moneychangers. But it didn't matter what they said. After a few of us men got over the shock, we were up on our feet headin' for them. By this point them Jesuses were doin' some sort of hustle dance. Absolute blasphemy.

Fred Konklin grabbed the first Jesus, a skinny little twerp with glasses, and piledrove him into the floor. Then the rest of the Jesuses scattered. But I kept my eyes on Chad. Even with the disguise, anybody could tell it was him with that long anglin' body. Could've played basketball had he been so inclined. Two more Jesuses were tackled and pummeled by the congregation. Men, women, and children all takin' turns on the whoopin'. Chad and a buddy slipped out the back door. By the time I made it to the parkin' lot, they were peelin' out in his Mustang. Me, Clifford Dobbs, and Sam Cantrell jumped into our trucks and pursued, pedal to the metal, chasin' those sons of bitches. We were takin' pop shots out the windows with our handguns. This is a right-to-carry state, and if you don't carry . . . well, that says a lot about your character.

Anyhow, tryin' to shoot left handed out a movin' vehicle on potholed streets ain't no easy feat, but Clifford managed to hit a back tire and send that 'Stang head-on into a telephone pole on Main and First. The passenger Jesus went out cold. Chad, the crazy fool that he was, climbed out with Bible in hand and shouted biblical passages while runnin' down Main. His robe flew open in the wind, showin' us his tighty-whiteys underneath. By this time a few other parishioners arrived, guns in hand, and well, it was a shootin' gallery. Seemed like we all got hits, but that bastard kept runnin' and bouncin' here and there after each bullet smack, wavin' his arms like a maniac. We had target practice on his movin' body.

Finally, he dropped to his knees, bleedin' from all them holes. He looked at us all and then up to the sky and said, "Forgive them for they know not what they do." He fell backwards, arms out like he was on a cross. Symbolic to the very end. We didn't say much, just stood there for several minutes with goose bumps on our arms.

We still don't talk about it much today. Some people, like my wife, think we did somethin' wrong, but it was blasphemy straight up. We'd've stoned him in Old Testament times. Besides, Chad was a liberal, and anybody who knows anything knows Jesus just wasn't that way. That's just common sense.

The Proxy

TREY TIVERTON SAT out on his front porch in his rocking chair, sipping from a jar of homemade hooch that was strong enough to melt the paint off of a barn. He watched a couple of his men play ping-pong in the afternoon shade of his barn-turned-lab. They'd snorted a little of the new batch and had excess energy to burn. They were smacking the dirty off-white ball nearly as fast as them Asians in the Olympics but with five times the mistakes. They should be using that energy to hunt down Owen Seaver, but then again they'd probably fuck it up and kill somebody innocent. Better to keep his muscle nearby, protecting the lab.

Owen was the junkie bastard who had stolen $1800 from him. Walking his useless ass three miles over to the homestead, he had acted like they were old friends again, and somehow, sentimentality and all that shit, Trey had let his guard down and allowed him inside the house where a stack of cash sat on the kitchen table.

Where Owen was hiding was anybody's guess, but Trey was certain he was still local. He never liked venturing too far from home. If that idiot had been any other tool in these parts, he'd have used that money to buy a jalopy and gotten the hell far away as possible from Lynchwood County. Of course the law was looking for him on the roads—an enemy of Trey was an enemy of the sheriff.

The rumble of BD's chopper let everybody in a square mile know he was coming. Trey didn't think it made much sense for his collections man to make such a loud entrance everywhere he went. Seemed like he should be all stealthy and sneak up on his prey like a copperhead on a rat. Didn't matter, though. BD, short for Bulldog (or Big Dick, so he says), always found who he sought, and they always paid what they owed and then some.

Clem and Jericho had stopped knocking that dirty plastic ball around and stood trembling. Could be the chemicals or could be fear. Trey imagined it was both.

BD pulled up the dirt driveway, dust trailing behind the two beasts, machine and man. The six-six giant wore a leather vest and leather pants in spite of the August heat. Prison ink covered his bulging arms with slogans and images that ran from his wrists up to his greasy overgrown beard. His Glock hung low from his belt like he was the gun-slinging Han Solo, but trapped in Chewbacca's body. When BD killed the engine, the earth stopped vibrating.

As he lumbered to Trey, it looked like he was trying to hold a poker face under his dark shades, but Trey could tell he was proud of something. And anything that made BD proud often included sadistic pain and suffering.

"You find 'im?" Trey asked, not moving an inch for his employee.

"Not yet, but don't worry none. You'll get his scalp soon enough." The beast pulled a wad of cash from his vest's inner pocket. It was sweaty and bloody.

"What's this for?" Trey asked, grabbing the money with the tips of his fingers.

"Jessup Watkins is paid up now."

Trey counted it out. Two hundred and forty. That was the right amount, less BD's twenty percent collection fee. Trey grabbed a notebook from a nearby table and wrote PAID next to Jessup's three-hundred-dollar debt. He should have asked for the entire three hundred and given the sixty back. This was some kind of test, Trey knew. He ought to nut up and remind the Neanderthal who was boss.

"How come the money's all bloody?" he asked instead.

BD grinned and pulled out a couple of broken teeth

from his pants pocket.

"Jessup's gonna find it a whole lot easier to whistle now," BD said with a grin.

Trey did his best not to show disgust. Couldn't show weakness around this brute. The sociopath intimidated everybody around him, and he'd had his eye on Trey's rocking chair for some time. Trey needed to flex some power, or BD would make his move sooner than later. The unbathed fool might have had the intimidating strength to run a drug operation, but not the brains to make it successful. He'd end up crippling or killing all his clients by the end of the year. And unable to pay off the law, he'd be a dead man before the spring. Trey hoped BD was smart enough to know he was an idiot.

"So what about Owen? You just goin' to let him walk around town?"

BD smiled through his crooked yellowed teeth. "Oh, that boy ain't struttin' around much. He's hidin' and layin' low. But he's gonna be appearin' around here real soon. I can guarantee it."

"What makes you so sure?"

"I had a talk with his gramps."

Trey's pulse quickened as he leaned forward in his chair. "You didn't hurt him, did you?"

BD shot his hands up in the air like he was an innocent angel. "I did no such thing. I heard you the first time, boss." He said "boss" like it was a disease.

"Well, what did you tell him then?"

"Oh, just how the longer Owen keeps hidin', the worse it'll be for him. Old man had tears streamin' down his face. Think he pissed himself too. Should've used Depends."

"Someone's comin'," Clem said from the barn. He and Jericho hadn't moved from the table, but hadn't resumed the game either. The ball's bounce sometimes got on BD's nerves, and nobody ever wanted to be in that spot.

The two tweakers brought out their pistols, and BD, spitting in the dirt, walked over to his hog to pick up his sawed-off. Most likely it was a client who ran across some cash and was ready to pound some crystal again. Occasionally, the Buckley boys came by, wanting to start some trouble. They manufactured meth too, but lower-grade shit. Chemical fiends avoided it if they could.

Trey felt safe about anybody gunning after him because they were going to have to do it head-on. Everybody knew the entire eighteen acres of Trey's unkempt farmland was booby-trapped.

When a familiar Chevy truck came down the dusty drive, Trey couldn't believe his eyes. It was old man Seaver. That degenerate Owen's grandfather.

BD walked over to Clem and Jericho. "Looks like we're catering to the senior citizens now," he said with a cruel smile. The tweakers laughed nervously.

"Ain't no way," Trey said, glaring at BD. "Mr. Seaver is straight as a ruler. Baptist through and through. Never touched a bottle in his life."

BD shrugged. "Whatever you say, boss."

Of course the same couldn't be said about Owen's mother, Angela. She'd drink, smoke, or snort anything in front of her. Even when Owen was a boy in the trailer with her. She eventually left Owen with his grandparents, took off to Houston, became a crack whore, and died of AIDS.

Mr. Seaver clambered out of his truck on thin, shaky legs. He had to be near eighty these days.

"The old coot needs a walker, don't he?"

The paddle-wielding tweakers laughed again.

"Shut it," Trey said, glaring at BD again. The tweakers looked down at their filthy shoes. BD glared back at Trey. There was gonna be a tussle between them real soon. Trey turned his attention back to feeble Mr. Seaver.

"Good afternoon, Mr. Seaver. What brings you over to my place?"

The old man kept walking with his head down until he reached the stairs. Sweat stained his faded denim shirt.

"Hey Gramps, my boss just asked you a question," BD

said just under a shout.

Mr. Seaver turned his head to the fierce brute, then looked up at Trey with bloodshot eyes behind thick, smudged glasses.

"Trey," he said with a tremor in his voice.

"That's Mr. Tiverton to you, old-timer," BD shouted, bounding over to him like a bouncer ready to break up a brawl.

The man trembled.

"I got this, BD," Trey said with his hand out to emphasize the point.

The collector spat and walked away from the porch, mumbling something about weakness. Trey felt like reaching behind the rocking chair, taking the shotgun strapped to the back of it, and blowing a hole through the ex-con . . . even if it meant spraying Clem and Jericho with some buckshot.

"How can I help you, Mr. Seaver?"

"Trey," Mr. Seaver said with an earnest face. "I need to ask you a favor."

"You know I can't afford to do favors around here. It's the nature of the business."

"I understand that, but what I was lookin' at doin' was payin' Owen's debt."

"I don't have no doubt that you intend to pay it, but I don't think you've got the means to pay it. You see, I'm not just talking about a loan or money owed. He stole a lot of money from me, Mr. Seaver, and I can't abide with that. I got a business to run, and reputation makes all the difference."

BD leaned against the weathered clapboards of the barn, causing them to groan. He crossed his arms and pointed his nose up to the sun as if he were looking down on this negotiation.

"What is it that you want from the boy exactly?" Mr. Seaver asked.

"Well, the money, for one thing," Trey said. He looked

over at his men, watching. He should send them on an errand, but what? Being the boss in the drug trade meant very little privacy. "But it's a bit more than that, you see? He stole, and a lesson has to be taught. People need to see that you don't mess with me."

"How much did he steal?"

"Eighteen hundred."

"Plus interest," BD said.

Trey shot him a glare. The brute spat, shaking his head.

"Good lord, that's about all I got, Trey," Mr. Seaver's voice cracked. He took a deep breath and reached for his back pocket.

Trey saw his men reach for their weapons, but he waved them off.

"Is a check all right?" the old man asked, pulling out a tattered checkbook. "You know I'm good for it."

"Yes, sir. But Mr. Seaver, you shouldn't be pay—"

"Yes, son. I gotta."

"It's not your problem. He done this to himself."

The old man shook his head. "I wasn't a good father."

Trey didn't know how he had raised Owen's mother, but he couldn't be held responsible for the wild child that she became. "Well, you were an excellent grandfather to Owen. And don't you believe anything different. You were good to me too, growin' up."

"Apparently I wasn't much good at that either," Mr. Seaver said, holding a stare through his murky glasses.

"Look now, you did us good. Real good. When I'd visit, you'd take us to movies, and fishin' and all that. Owen and I loved bein' around you. Don't you think no different, understand?"

"Well, look at how you turned out. I mean . . ." Mr. Seaver held his head down, shaking it. Unlike BD, there was no anger, but defeat and sadness in the headshake.

"Mr. Seaver, you can't take responsibility for the way we turned out. I mean, in some ways I'm kind of a success, you know. Entrepreneurial, runnin' my own business and such."

"But Owen . . ."

"Owen was the one who started me in this trade. He learned the formulas from someplace, and I did the business end. We were partners, but . . ." Trey stopped and bit his lip for a second. He would not allow his voice to break with his crew close by. "Owen couldn't keep from using the product and bein' a liability. He's an addict, like his mom. Must be in his genes."

"It's in the genes, all right. My daddy was an alcoholic. Had an awful temper in him when he was drinkin'. I never touched the evil stuff."

There was a long pause. The breeze rattled the leaves of the surrounding trees.

"So can you tell me what else is owed?" Mr. Seaver said, finally breaking the silence.

"Retribution." The word slipped out before Trey could stop himself. It was true, though. Money alone wasn't enough to even out the theft.

"A butt-kicking?" the old man asked.

Clem and Jericho chuckled.

"A little more than that. Like lyin'-in-bed-for-a-few-weeks kind of punishment." Mr. Seaver took in Trey's words, nodding thoughtfully. "I wouldn't kill him though. Who knows, he might even dry out in the hospital."

"Would you knock out his teeth? I hear that big one likes to collect 'em," he said with a nervous glance to BD.

"If it happens with a punch or a kick, then yes. But I won't let anybody take a pair of pliers to his mouth. You gotta understand, things will get broken, Mr. Seaver. They have to."

"And then it's even. Owen is free and clear. Clean slate?"

Trey looked over at his men. The tweakers were doing their best to stand still while the brute basked in a patch of sunlight like a reptile.

After finding out that the money was missing, Trey had wanted Owen slaughtered. The betrayal was too much. He'd wanted Owen brutalized within an inch of life, and then after BD had extracted all of the pain that one could from a human body, he'd snuff out his former best friend's life. But Trey's outrage was mellowing, and now he reckoned a lesson was enough.

"Slate will be clean. You have my word."

Mr. Seaver pulled out a pen from his front pocket and wrote out an $1800 check out to cash. He handed it to Trey with a trembling hand.

"So we're half done here, you understand? Owen still needs to show up. We won't be gentle, but one of us will drop him off at the hospital alive. I swear on my parents' grave."

Mr. Seaver nodded. His face had paled to a waxy sheen. He ambled back to his truck, but then stopped and turned around. "Trey."

"Yes, sir."

"Lemme stand in for him."

"Excuse me?"

"Proxy. Let me proxy for my grandson."

"What the hell's a proxy?" BD asked.

Trey was about to speak, but held his tongue. He knew what it was, sort of.

"It's like a substitute," Mr. Seaver told BD.

"Mr. Seaver, this isn't your—"

"You mean we can kick your ass on account of your no-good grandson?" BD interrupted.

Mr. Seaver nodded his head gravely. BD let out a cruel laugh.

"Dammit, Mr. Seaver, you shouldn't be takin' no beating on account of a thievin' junkie. Ever," Trey said. "I've already taken all your money."

"He's my grandson, my only one. The crap that goes into his body . . . well, it may make him a different person sometimes, but it don't change who he is to me." He walked up to the porch, his eyes steady on Trey. "I ain't got much time left on this planet anyhow, and if this is something I can do for Owen, well . . ."

The man's lower lip trembled, but he had determination behind his pale blue eyes. Trey saw BD nearly salivating while the tweakers scratched themselves, unsure of what to do.

"I can't, Mr. Seaver. I'm sorry." If they were alone, Trey might have called everything even. But he couldn't with his men around.

"Yes, you can. You gotta kick my butt for him."

"It's not your punishment to take."

"I'm Owen's proxy. You gotta give it to me."

"You won't survive."

"I'm a hell of a lot stronger than you think. You . . . you no-good twerp." Mr. Seaver spat on the porch step, just below Trey's boots.

"Are you disrespecting my boss?" BD said in his booming voice.

"And your mother," Mr. Seaver said. "You shoulda seen the damage I done to her last night."

Clem let out a laugh, and BD clocked him on the back of the head. He moved toward the old man. Trey knew it would be hard to stop the charging rhino.

"Mr. Seaver, don't be escalatin' this situation here."

"Oh, screw yourself, Trey. You're nothin' more than a disease in this county. A plague rottin' the futures of men, women, and children. A filthy, disgustin' disease."

In spite of himself, Trey flew down the steps and grabbed Mr. Seaver by his shirt. He was lighter than he had imagined. Mr. Seaver looked at Trey with raised eyebrows that showed hope, but then dropped to disappointment when Trey loosened his grip.

"And you're a coward too," Mr. Seaver said. "A weak little boy who used to get scared of grass snakes in trees. You can't keep runnin' an outfit like this."

The old man hawked a wad of spit in Trey's face. Trey

decked him before he could stop himself. Mr. Seaver dropped to the dirt like a pile of wet rags. BD whooped. He and the junkies were on the senior citizen in seconds, kicking the shit out of him. Trey wiped the spit off his face and came to his senses.

"Hold up now. I said stop it!"

Trey yanked his .38 revolver from the back of his waistband and blasted it in the air.

The beating stopped. Trey looked down at the broken figure below covered in dust and blood. So much damage in under thirty seconds.

"Is he still alive?" he asked.

Clem dropped to the ground, putting his ear on Mr. Seaver's mouth. "The geezer's still breathin'!"

"That's Mr. Seaver, Clem."

"One stomp on his head, and I can take him out of his misery," BD said.

Trey couldn't hold back a shiver. "Leave him alone, BD," he said with a crack in his voice. "And give him space to breathe, all of ya, dammit."

"I think he's sayin' somethin'," Clem said.

Trey fell to his knees. "Mr. Seaver, are you all right?"

Something raspy and guttural came out of his bloody lips.

"What's that?" Trey said, straining to listen.

"Are we . . . even . . . Trey?"

"Yes, sir. Slate's clean." Trey put his hand on the man's trembling body.

The faintest smile broke across the old man's lips as he closed his eyes, his body going slack.

"Clem, Jericho. Get Mr. Seaver to the hospital." The tweakers looked at Trey, confused. "Take his truck. Go!"

Clem hefted Mr. Seaver by his shoulders while Jericho grabbed his ankles.

"Be careful, now," Trey called after them.

"It don't matter none," BD said.

Trey turned to the beast, wanting to pull out his .38

again. "What's that supposed to mean?"

"This is the way he wanted to go out. The old coot thinks he sacrificed himself for his jonesin' grandson. I imagine he'll die today or tomorrow thinkin' he bought Owen some clemency." BD spat. "Damn old fool."

Trey watched Jericho back the old truck down the drive while Clem held Mr. Seaver's limp, bloody body up on the bench seat.

"You know Owen will be comin' back here," Trey said.

"Whatchya gonna do about it?" BD asked.

Trey chewed his lip. He'd been a man of his word, even as a drug dealer. But no man should ever proxy for Owen, especially somebody as blameless as Mr. Seaver.

"We spilled innocent blood today." Trey looked at BD.

BD shrugged. "He asked for it. I don't feel bad at all." He put his hands on his hips. "And if you want my opinion—"

"I don't," interrupted Trey.

"You got too much morality to be slingin' drugs in these parts. You should be workin' in a library or some-thin'."

"Is that so?"

"Yep."

"And I suppose you're the one who thinks he oughta take over my operations if I were to leave the business, huh?"

That cruel smile spread across BD's lips. Was this it, the final throwdown? Trey's body steeled, ready to pull out his .38 and end this bullshit here and now. BD's Glock hung off his belt, his hand hanging in the nearby vicinity. This was a modern-day showdown in the backwoods. They glared at each other, holding their stares. BD licked his lips, anticipation in his eyes. Yeah, it was on.

There was the sound of something coming up the drive, but neither man turned to look. A sideways glance equaled a death sentence. Trey was already at a disadvantage with his warm pistol tucked behind his waistband. He'd have to reach behind and pull it out as fast as possible to beat BD. One mistake, and it was all over.

A skinny body on a bike appeared in Trey's peripheral vision.

"Whassup Trey, BD?" a familiar voice shouted out.

Trey blinked. Fucking Owen Seaver. BD's shoulders relaxed an inch.

"What're you doing here, Owen? You know you shouldn't be showin' your face in these parts, ever," Trey said, still keeping his eyes on BD.

"Well, the way I hear it, we're good now."

Both Trey and BD turned to the skeletal addict on an undersized purple bike with streamers hanging off the handlebars. Somewhere out there, a girl was crying, missing her ride.

"And how did you hear that?" BD asked.

"I saw Jericho drivin' Grandpa's truck down the road. I waved him down and got the whole story." Owen gave that ugly yellow meth smile. "We're even-stevens now, man."

"So you were waiting down the road for your grandfather to plead your case, huh?" Trey said, feeling an anger swell up. "You asked him to come out here, didn't you?"

Owen shrugged. "A deal's a deal, right? You've always been true to your word, Trey." Nothing but hunger lingered in those desperate eyes. He only wanted to score, that was it. Didn't care a whit about his granddad.

"How was he doing when you saw him?" Trey asked.

"What's that?"

"Your grandfather. You know, the guy who proxied for you?"

"You boys done kicked the shit out of him," Owen said, shaking his head and smiling. "Sure glad that wasn't me." He reached into filthy denim pockets and pulled out a wad of cash. A portion of what he'd stolen from Trey, no doubt. "How about you score me three grams. Your shit's better than the Buckley brothers'."

Trey glanced over at BD. He arched his eyebrows, and Trey knew what he was thinking. He might well have asked, *What're you going to do about this, boss man?*

"How's your tooth collection, BD?"

"I could use a few more."

"Well, go get yourself some more then."

BD smiled. Not his cruel grin, but one of respect. "Sure thing, boss."

Trey sauntered back to the porch, feeling the urge for a sip of hooch.

"Hey now, Trey. A deal's a deal," Owen cried before taking the first blow.

Cop in a Well

YOU KNEW YOU should've called for backup when Little Don and Eugene Everett asked you to stop by their place around one in the morning. At least you'd thought enough about the situation to strap a backup .22 in one boot and a switchblade in the other. Neither helped you though when Eugene pointed at a computer monitor and asked you to watch grainy security video footage of yourself putting a tracking device under one of their mobile meth-lab trailers, and Little Don snuck up from behind, conking you on the head with an aluminum bat.

You wake up, lying in the bed of Eugene's F-150 bouncing down a dirt road. Your hands and legs are duct-taped tight, and your throbbing head screams out in pain. The shocks on this truck are busted, and Eugene seems to intentionally hit every pothole and rock. Looking up at the cold stars above, you have a lonesome, sinking feeling that this is your last night on earth.

After they haul you out of the truck bed and drop you on the hard ground, the two brothers start kicking you with their pointy-toe boots and shouting that you're worse than a pile of crap.

"Nothin' I hate more than a narc," Eugene says.

"If I had my way I'd just shoot you dead, but Daddy don't want it that way," Little Don says.

"Regardless, it sucks for you. Big time, bro," Eugene adds with a malignant smile. Even in the blue moonlight, you can see the yellow film on his tobacco-stained teeth.

Their daddy is Big Don Everett, son of a long line of moonshiners. Over the years the family business expanded into weed and now meth. The Everett clan is infamous in the region, and not a single member in the history of the family has ever been known to have a high IQ. Yet after decades of trying, the law has never been able to bust any of them on a significant charge.

You're an undercover cop who volunteered to infiltrate this notorious family enterprise and find out what happened to a deputy who went missing more than a year ago. Now you're up for a quick, unwanted retirement.

The brothers pick up your bruised and bleeding body, and haul you over to an old stone well. You kick and buck as hard as you can, but both of these boys are big and have strong, unyielding grips. You'd rather take a bullet to the brain than drown in darkness. At this point you'd compromise anything and everything not to die this way: who's in charge of the investigation, the intel that has been reported on the family, your Social Security number, email and ATM passwords. Just name it. But you can't, because duct tape was slapped across your mouth when they first tossed you in the truck.

"Look at 'im kick like a mule," Little Don says.

"Dumbshit thinks he's gonna drown."

You pause for a millisecond's worth of confusion, and they fling you into the hole. Falling into pitch blackness, the tumble seems infinite until you smack with a thud into soft, wet mud. The breath is knocked out of your lungs and your shoulder aches something horrible, but the rest of you seems to be okay. You had worse beatings when you went undercover as a bouncer a few years back. Best of all, you realize, there isn't enough water to drown. Flopping on your back, you look up to the weak moonlight above— maybe twenty-five, thirty feet up—and see the black silhouettes of the two boys. Their laughter echoes.

"See you later, narc," Eugene says.

Seconds later, you hear his truck rumble to life and leave. Total darkness surrounds you, and the cold, damp air smells putrid. You struggle to get the boot off your foot, as your ankles are taped. Finally, the right one comes free. With your hands behind your back, you feel inside the boot, finding the inner sleeve with the hidden switchblade. Thank God the brothers didn't frisk you very well, taking only your cell phone and the Glock you had tucked into the back of your jeans. Working the blade on the tape, you get it to tear enough that you can break it apart in spite of your sore shoulder. Hands free, you take the tape off your mouth and shout for help. From the roughness of the road, you know you're nowhere near civilization, but you can't help shouting until your voice hurts.

After the tape is stripped off your ankles and the little .22 backup pistol from your other boot is shoved into your back pocket, you crawl around in slimy mud, touching what has to be a body, twice in separate directions. Freaked out, you reach up for the ceiling of the well. Your hands wave in the air, touching nothing. The thick, suctioning mud doesn't allow you to jump an inch. There is nothing you can do, so you decide to sit in the moonlight rays, listening to the gentle sway of the oaks. Just conserve your energy for now and wait for the light of day.

* * *

YOU WAKE WITH a start, hearing truck doors slam shut. Crawling out of the sunlight, you wait for them, pistol aimed at the top of the stone-lined well. The pistol's not accurate at long distances and there are only five rounds in the magazine, but nothing would make you feel better than to pop one of those sons of bitches before you die down here.

"Here piggy-piggy-piggy," Little Don says with his deep voice, followed by a cruel laugh.

Both of their heads peer over the edge of the well. Setting the sights on Eugene, you see him holding something in his hand. A stick.

"We thought you might like to know that you ain't down there all alone." Eugene's ears look big enough to cover the well.

"Take a look at your neighbors," Little Don says, wearing his filthy, faded orange Volunteers hat backwards as he always does.

Eugene strikes the stick against the rock wall, and a bright red flame sparks. He drops the road flare into the hole. It falls three feet in front of you. You are blinded for half a second, but as soon as your vision returns you take the shot. A mortared stone bursts in front of Eugene as he jerks back, screaming. You aim at Little Don's fat head, but he's vanished.

You pick up the flare and sweep it around the well. To your surprise it's a wide, open cavern. Probably eight feet tall with a diameter of—and that's when you see them. All of them. Bodies. Some skeletons, some still decomposing. Seven or eight at least. You are frozen, shocked with horror. Then a bullet rips the air past your ear. You run from the opening of the hole while Little Don curses your name and blasts gunfire from above. You dash out the flare into the mud, hoping you can reignite it another time.

You creep back to the edge of the hole with your little pistol raised, but Little Don is no longer there. You hear him shout from above, "We'll be back for you . . . you fuckin' narc! And we're gonna make you pay big time." As if they were easy on you and weren't making you pay enough already. A smile creases your lips as you realize you must have harmed Eugene pretty good. While it's not equal justice for their slow murder of you, it's better than nothing.

You don't want to, but you search the bodies for a lighter. It is disgusting work, but you tell yourself this is about survival. Most of the corpses still have their arms taped behind their backs. What a horrible way to die.

Eventually you find a Zippo stamped with a rebel flag in one of the corpse's pockets and relight the flare. You count ten bodies. Hovering over each of them, they all have identifying human characteristics even in rotting decomposition. You don't recognize anybody. None of them are the missing deputy. The bodies no longer bother you as much now that you've been up close and personal with them. What bothers you are the things moving in the shadows. Creepy crawlies like spiders and salamanders.

Unfortunately, the man-made rock lining the well is too far out of reach for you to grab a handhold and climb out of this death trap. You suppose the well had been dug at least a century back, if not two. You wonder if the diggers had abandoned the project after coming upon this foul, muddy water, or if they threw in a pail and started drinking. Mission accomplished. We got water! Drinking this foul stuff would explain why the Everett clan is so screwed up.

You trudge through ankle-deep mud towards a dark corner. There is a crack in the limestone wall. A slim crevice you might be able to squeeze through. It'll be a tight fit, and you could easily get stuck in there, trapped for the rest of your life. Or maybe, impossibly, you might slither through and find an escape.

Salamanders dart away as you crawl through, following a path zigging left and then right. The blinding red flare spits painful molten flames on your hand. The space above opens up to at least a twenty-foot ceiling, allowing you to stand and walk through the crevice. Upon turning another corner you find a solid, slick limestone wall dead-ending the path. And there is another disturbing discovery. At the base of the rock is a corpse wearing a sheriff's uniform.

You know who it is without checking his ID. Deputy Nick Rogers. You were the best man at his wedding. When he told you about the drug trafficking happening in his county, you told the brave officer to contact the Nashville DEA. Then a few weeks later he disappeared from sight. His wife, Lori, was pregnant and worried out of her skull. You were determined to go undercover and find out what happened to your best friend. Resting your hand on his shoulder, you say a prayer and wish Nick peace in the afterlife.

* * *

YOU SEARCH EVERY angle of this cavernous well until the neon-red flame of the flare shrinks dangerously close to your fingers. You reckon the width is about the size of a baseball diamond. Sitting under the well's opening where daylight penetrates and warms a circular spot in the vast damp darkness, you know you will need to conserve your energy. The Everett boys will come back. They have to. Their pride dictates that they must have the final word on everything.

There is a churning in your stomach that you try to ignore. Although you're starving, you're not ready to turn cannibal. At least not yet. Then you hear the rumble of a truck approaching. Diesel-powered. Three cab doors slam shut. Backing up into the dark shadows, you aim your pistol at the bright round sky.

Three men peek quickly into the hole and pull their heads back, much like prairie dogs or Whac-A-Mole. The three are Little Don, Eugene with a bandage over his eye, and a bearded hillbilly named Rexford Everett. His mangy salt-and-pepper beard hangs at least two feet below his chin, covering the bib on his overalls. The boys call him Uncle Rex.

"Hey, Nathan, or whatever your real name is," the uncle says. "You think you can just take out my nephew's eye and not get payback from us, you got another thing comin'."

"It's payback time, you . . . you son of a bitch," Eugene says, spitting out his anger.

None of them keep their heads over the hole long enough to get a good shot.

"Burn 'im, Uncle Rex," Little Don says.

"Fire in the hole!" the uncle yells, and a gasoline-filled Jack Daniel's bottle with a burning rag on top falls from the opening. You jump back, but the Molotov cocktail lands with a thud in the muck, right-side up, and very much intact with the rag still burning.

"What happened, Uncle Rex?" Eugene asks.

"Dunno," Rex says.

Adrenaline surges through your body as you rush toward the cocktail and hurl it up at the opening with all your might. At that exact moment, all three men crane their necks over the edge of the well. The bottle smashes against the upper, rock lined edge and explodes into a mighty fireball. The men holler in surprise and pain. Flames engulf Rex's long beard.

"Get it out! Get it out!" he shouts.

The boys are screaming in agony too. You saw Eugene's bandages catch fire as well as Little Don's ratty Volunteers hat. Balls of fire and pieces of glass fall down at your feet.

There are multiple curses and shouts before the truck engine turns over with a deep rumble that quickly fades away.

* * *

YOU WAIT FOR two days for them to come back again. You've lived on a diet of spiders, salamanders, and pale insects you don't want to think about too much. The good thing is that those critters are high in protein. Enough to keep you alive and alert. You now know the well's cavern intimately, having mapped in your mind all the nooks and crannies by touch. You spend most of your time, however, by the hole waiting. The Everetts will come back. They have to. Revenge is ingrained in their inbred DNA. They neither forgive nor forget the slightest slights they've ever received, going back for generations.

When you finally hear an approaching vehicle, you identify at least two rumbling engines, one having the deep bass of Big Don's half-ton dually. Big Don is the operator of the family enterprise, an empire that keeps all their neighbors impoverished, addicted, and frightened.

In a kneeling position, you steady your aim, ready to take out the head of this corrupt organization with the pop gun. Instead, a pair of Uzis appear on opposite sides of the well and begin rapid-firing. You roll away as mud flies everywhere. A burst of bullets pummel the soft earth, puncturing it relentlessly and creating a crater in the well's light. A defined no man's land that you cannot enter. There is no way you'll get a shot at Big Don. Finally, the barrage stops.

"Hey, Nathan the Narc, down there," Big Don says in his twangy baritone voice. "I want you to know, right here, right now, that these are your last few minutes on earth. Hear me? Eugene here lost an eye 'cause of you. My brother's in ICU sufferin' from first-degree burns all over his face 'cause of you. And Little Don's suffered some major burns too."

"I'm fine, Dad," Little Don says.

"You're never gonna grow hair on the top of your head again, son."

You can't help but smile.

"You're gonna burn in hell, you son of a bitch," a woman shouts from above. It's Mary-Jo Everett, Big Don's wife and treasurer of this family-run drug empire. She's also his cousin. Didn't even have to change her name when they wed. You looked at their family tree, and a lot of branches kept looping back around.

You want to get close to the opening just to get a peek at Little Don's bandaged head, but you know Uzis are trained on the hole, ready to strike. Still, it might be worth it.

"If there's one thing I hate most, it's a traitor. The way you came in all smooth and snake-like, doin' us favors, tradin' cigarettes for hooch and meth. That's wrong to trick a man like that, you duplee-tish-us son of a bitch. I guess it don't matter much now, anyway. Your time on this earth ends today."

Big Don talks with so much bluster, you wonder what

he could have in store for you. Edging just a little closer, fully automatic gunfire blasts from above with all the fury of mechanized hell. You dive backwards into the muck. Turning, you see a large bundle of sticks—red sticks taped together like flares, but bigger—fall into the crater. A couple of wires hang from the top of the hole to the package of sticks. Your breath catches as you realize it's not a bundle of flares. It's dynamite. A lot of dynamite. More than what's needed to kill you. It's enough to take out the side of a mountain.

Heart pounding, you scramble for the crevice. It's dark, but you know where it is at as you step over the bodies. Inside the fissure, you turn left, then right, working your way through the zigzag maze. When you reach the dead end with Nick's corpse, you huddle in the corner, pulling your friend and fallen hero on top of you for protection.

The explosion is tremendous. It shakes the world above, below, and to the side of you. The heat from the dynamite singes your clothes, and then dirt and debris rains on top of you from the cavernous ceiling above. Piles of it, nearly crushing you to death.

Gasping for air, you push up with your legs like you're doing squats at the gym with too many weights. Nick's body slides off your shoulders and heavy chunks of dirt fall in his place. You thrust your arms up, pushing them through the soil. Grasping dirt, you pull and kick, wiggling your body upward through the dirt as debris fills in under your feet. You keep doing this. It's like swimming a complicated breaststroke through a thick soup filled with ball bearings. It feels like you are making progress. The weight of the dirt lightens, but you need air real bad.

Your right hand reaches out and touches a limestone wall. The edge of it. You kick the soil madly, working your body toward it. Pushing up on the ledge and putting your foot on the wall, you use your last bit of energy to shove up. Dirty sunlight comes into view as you gasp, sucking in dirt and oxygen.

Hacking up dirt, you pull your body half out of the baking hot ground. You wheeze, coughing and inhaling air. Sunlight pierces your eyes, blinding you. You can't see anything, but you don't care. You just need air. All of it, right now, in your lungs.

Through a smoky haze of dust floating in the air, the light blue sky is the most beautiful thing you've ever seen in your life. Then you glance around, and what you see doesn't register, at least not at first. The scene before you looks nothing like Tennessee, but more like a war zone featured on the news or the History Channel.

The well is totally obliterated. A cavernous hole in the ground looks like a bomb had been dropped from a B-52 thousands of feet in the air. Black twisting smoke still wafts in the air around it. Following the radius of the blast, it looks like the crevice and the twisting limestone maze tempered the explosion's impact, saving you from complete annihilation.

Then you wonder about the Everetts. Did they have enough common sense to run for the hills to try to survive? Or were they swallowed up in the destruction too? You don't see them anywhere, although Mary-Jo's pink Escort has flipped over, resting on its side like a sleeping piglet. Besides blown-out windows, Big Don's heavy-duty dually seems to be intact. Then you look up at the scorched oaks and find them. Parts of them, anyway.

Swaying from the branches, you see a random leg here, an arm there. Bits and pieces of Everetts everywhere. You identify one of the oversized gold rings that Big Don used to wear from a severed hand, as well as a spiderweb tattoo Eugene had inked on his right calf.

Crawling the rest of the way out of the hole and onto the seared grass, you limp over to Big Don's truck. It's not in as good of shape as you believed. It looks as if it has rolled over once or twice, but somehow managed to land back on its wheels. It takes a few pulls, but you get the door open. Keys dangle from the ignition. A dirt-caked smile spreads across your lips. Man, you're going to have one crazy, messed-up story to tell your law enforcement buddies and the brass back in Nashville.

For several generations, nobody could stop the Everetts. Anybody who came close disappeared, only to now be vaporized. In all honesty, you can't even take credit for wiping that clan out. The only people on earth capable of ending the Everett reign of terror were the Everetts themselves. And they did it with one big bang.

A Bro Code Violation

A FEW MINUTES before dusk, Wade heard the crunch of
dead, frozen leaves and the snap of twigs coming his way.
From his perch in the treestand, he pointed his .30-06
toward the trail as his finger eased on the trigger. His heart
thumped. It could be either a deer or Bill, ready to call it a
day. It would be just his luck if it were a deer. Squinting
through the scope, he saw an orange vest and hesitated.
What if it were somebody else? This was public land.

"You about ready to head home?" Bill shouted. "I'm
freezin' my nuts off."

Wade saw Bill had more orange than when they had
first entered the woods. Flecks of neon cheese crumbs
littered his beard and his fingers. Probably a bag of
Cheetos lay under a tree with two discarded forty-ounce
bottles of Buds. Such a degenerate. No wonder Tessa
wanted him gone. Why she had chosen him over Wade six
years ago still made no sense. His finger twitched on the
trigger.

"What, you think I'm deer? Ain't got no horns, bro."

Wade lowered the rifle and pushed the safety. He
couldn't do it. Not with Bill looking at him with that
dopey, aw-shucks expression. Grabbing his pack wedged
under his treestand, he climbed two branches down to the
hard, half-frozen ground. What the hell was he going to
tell Tessa? *Sorry, I left your husband alive on our hunting trip.
Maybe I'll shoot him next time.* Tessa, with her fiery temper,
would probably call him weak and threaten to find another
man with bigger balls. That same weakness had afflicted
Wade's entire life: no follow-through on his desires.

"Didn't see a damn thing," Bill said, shaking his head. "How about you?"

"Nothin'," Wade said.

"I swear, hunting ain't nothing more than freezin' and drinkin'. Or is it drinkin' and freezin'?" He belched and smiled, so proud of himself. "Speakin' of which, I say we head over to Slim's before happy hour's over."

"Sure thing."

"Besides, I ain't in no hurry to get home. Tessa'll be bitchin' about something I forgot to do." Bill spat, his chubby face tightening with disgust. "I'm tellin' you, there ain't no way to satisfy that woman."

Wade shook, but it wasn't from the chilly twenty-five degrees. He just needed to do this. Turn off his conscience, raise his Winchester, and blow a hole through his child-hood friend. Why was he hesitating? He and Tessa had planned this out for over a month now. *Just do it, you coward.*

"Gotta take a leak first," Bill said, walking toward a patch of saplings. "Water these here trees. Goin' green with a little bit of my yellow. Environmentalists oughta love me."

Wade shook his head. The idiot was making this too easy. Gripping his rifle, he felt his hands moisten with sweat inside his Thinsulate gloves.

"Hey, what's this over here?"

Bill found it. The four-foot-deep grave Wade had had the foresight to dig a couple of weeks earlier before the freeze made everything rock-hard solid. Even then the ground hadn't been very soft.

"Whatcha looking at?" Wade said, trying to sound natural.

"This," Bill said, working his way to the hole that was about twenty yards from the big tree. He walked toward it in a clumsy, lumbering stride. The sun was setting, and everything seemed to be covered with a gauzy layer of gray. "Looks like somebody wants to bury a body."

Bringing the walnut stock to his shoulder, Wade pushed the safety off.

"Can you step two paces to your left."

"What?" Bill said, turning around.

The whites of Bill's eyes widened when Wade squeezed the trigger. A bright orange flash lit up the nearby trees and saplings, followed by a thunderous boom and a solid kick in his shoulder. Bill jerked back, dropping his beloved Remington 770, and clutched the center of his chest where a reddening puncture grew. Confusion clouded Bill's face as he stumbled backward. He didn't fall into the hole, but landed a few feet away from it in the clearing. Close enough to roll Bill's thick body into it without much effort. *Thanks, bro.*

Wade waited. He heard his friend's final gasping breaths, but didn't want to see it. A mixture of exhilaration and horror rushed through his body. He'd done it. Bill was permanently out of Tessa's life. They might have to wait a little while to go public, but he and Tessa could be together without the shame of a divorce and all of that. It felt good that it was finally over. Mostly.

It grew darker and colder while Wade gave Bill's soul a few extra minutes to leave the earth. He glanced at his Timex. 5:08. He drew in a deep breath and crossed over the saplings to Bill, whose open eyes faced the sky and brow was still knit with bewilderment.

Bill's round body collected leaves and branches as Wade push-rolled it into the grave. *Just like Bill*, Wade thought, looking at the corpse covered in earth and grime. *A pathetic mess to the very end.*

Shaking his head, he removed the Army surplus fold-up shovel from his pack. He stood over Bill's body, trembling.

"Why'd you hafta go an' marry Tessa, jackass? You knew I still loved her, even after we broke up for a spell. That wasn't right."

He threw a spade full of dirt on Bill's stupid face. Chucks of earth bounced off his forehead and slid down into his greasy hair. Tessa had wanted to marry Wade. Put pressure on him to ask, but he just wasn't ready yet. So they broke up. Wade needed a little space, some time to think. But then Bill swooped down like a hawk circling an open-air chicken farm. Bastard.

One measly toss at a time, Wade kept scooping and dumping. This was taking longer than expected. Wade hadn't brought a full-sized shovel because he didn't want to draw Bill's suspicion and have to answer his dumbass questions about why he was driving around in the middle of winter with a shovel. He could hear Bill declare, "Ain't nobody diggin' holes when it's this cold, bro."

Wade shook his head. So what? He should have come up with some excuse to appease Bill. Anything, really. His friend would've been dumb enough to believe it. Wade swore to himself. He was suffering the consequences, yet again, from overthinking. That overcautious, overplanning brain of his that had to overanalyze every possible angle. Sometimes he thought so much that it led to near paralysis. That's how Tessa slipped through his fingers and into Bill's impulsive, I'm-taking-what's-in-front-of-me, meaty paws.

Stupid. Stupid. Stupid.

Wade was more than halfway finished with the burial when he remembered Bill's Remington. He found the bolt action after a quick search. Hesitating, he held it over the hole, unable to let go. It was a nice rifle, but that Leupold scope was even better. Wade squeezed his eyes shut and shook his head. What the hell was he thinking? He didn't kill his best friend for profit. Nope, not at all. He wasn't a thief. His motivation was true. This murder was for love, pure and simple. He dropped the rifle into the pit.

The lingering light of the day was no more than a fading candle in the west. The darkest shade of navy blue was surrounded by blackness with the billions of white pinholes. The bitter cold that Wade had endured all day was turning into hypothermic freezing as the dry arctic breeze from the north picked up strength with bone-piercing gusts. Wade's toes, fingers, and nose felt numb, but his back and arms ached something fierce. The pile of loose dirt he'd shoveled weeks earlier grew harder as his spade dug closer to the ground. Wade strained his eyes, teary from the wind, to see what was in front of him. Good enough, he decided. He patted down Bill's grave, trying to make it smooth and natural.

Wade tensed for a quarter of a second when a vision of Bill's arm shooting out of the ground and grabbing hold of his ankle seized his brain. He laughed it off. When was the last time he'd eaten? Just two packages of beef jerky since this morning's breakfast. He imagined a bowl of Tessa's hot and tasty venison stew with Tessa sitting across a table from him, wearing a loose robe with nothing underneath. She reaches across a table, exposing her soft breasts, and feeds him a chunk of warm, delicious cornbread. With a tender look of satisfaction in her eyes, she takes his hand, leading him to his bedroom. A smile crossed Wade's chapped lips. Yes, Tessa was worth killing for.

Wade scooped up branches and leaves as fast as he could, tossing them over the grave. He needed to get out of there, find some cell phone reception, and let Tessa know he'd done it. Then he would collect his reward. Even in the dark, Wade felt pretty certain no random hunters would take notice of this spot the next day or week, or even a year from now. But he'd come back tomorrow, just to be sure.

He grabbed his pack and rifle before working his way down the trail. Wade pushed Bill out of his mind, focusing on Tessa and their future together. But that made him think of the time lost. Why hadn't he taken out Bill earlier? There had been plenty of opportunities. How many chances had he had to push a drunken Bill, rod and reel in hand, out of his aluminum boat or let the jackass drive home, three sheets to the wind, instead of wrestling his keys away?

Wade had walked a quarter of a mile before he realized he'd been trudging in the wrong direction. Just getting deeper into the woods. Of all the things he'd prepared, a flashlight wasn't one of them. He turned around, retracing his steps. When he finally reached the open field, it was already after seven. Making out the outline of his Chevy Silverado on the road was like finding a pop machine in the desert. He had three things on his mind: warmth, food, and Tessa. Then fear struck Wade. He patted his front pockets. Nothing but his Buck knife. He dropped the Winchester and his pack, running his gloved hands all over himself hoping to find them somewhere else. Nothing.

"Bill, you . . . you . . . stupid fat idiot motherfucker." He screamed at the rising moon. How could he have been so stupid to forget? Bill had come by around noon wanting the keys because he was "gettin' the munchies." Wade had tossed them down from the tree, unnerved to see his friend before dusk, the appointed killing time, and eagerly shooed him away.

Wade pulled on the door handle, hoping that Bill might have done him an unintended favor by leaving it unlocked like he often had with his own F-150. But the alarm beeped angrily. Wade stepped back. The last thing he wanted to do was to trip the alarm and have a game warden bust him for hunting after hours. Besides, he hadn't told anybody he was hunting. He was supposed to be up north, checking up on his granddad in the nursing home.

Wade ran his hands over his head. He knew he wasn't the smartest guy in town, but hanging out with Bill, he must have tricked himself into believing he was.

"How could I be such a fucking idiot?" he shouted.

He glanced at his cell phone, no bars. And there wouldn't be for at least another three miles. He looked into the sheer darkness of the woods. He'd have to go back, find Bill's grave, and unbury that keys-stealing bastard.

* * *

WADE'S EYES ADJUSTED enough to spot big solid objects like tree trunks, but he couldn't see the branches that scratched his face. He wasn't even sure if he was on the trail. He powered forward, trying to find the spot: the tree he had stood under when he'd murdered his best friend. He exhaled. Tessa was worth it, right? He chuckled softly, realizing he'd violated Bill's first rule in the bro code, "No hoes before bros." Wade's eyes watered, but he told himself it was because of that damn dry Arctic wind.

It took about two hours of circling, snapping through branches, and tripping over rocks before he found the tree. He knew it was the right one because he'd left the treestand behind. Good Lord, he was sloppy. But then again, it wasn't every day that you kill your best friend. At least this mistake paid off.

An intense shiver took hold of him. His teeth clattered uncontrollably. The wind-chill factor made the single-digit temperature feel like negative fifteen. He realized he was also dehydrated, having tasted the last drops of black coffee back when there was daylight. But that wasn't the main reason he was shaking. It was the task that lay ahead. Wade gripped the oak's bark for support. A few yards beyond the tree lay Bill Moody. Best friend and biggest idiot in the world. Why'd that dipshit choose Tessa? So many other women liked him in spite of his lard ass and crudeness. It was that whole personality thing. Something Wade sorely knew he lacked.

He looked at this watch. Already 9:30.

"Get with it, coward," he whispered to himself.

He dropped his pack and pulled out the shovel. He paced twenty yards like he was a football official marking off a personal foul plus five extra. The ground finally seemed to soften. Wade looked down, not seeing anything but knowing that Bill was underneath. Thoughts of the past invaded Wade's mind. The two boys fishing in the creek with a string of perch, camping in the woods, getting kicked out of Boy Scouts for locking the Scoutmaster in the latrine. Nausea overcame Wade, but he couldn't afford to vomit. He was already weak and shivering like a newborn pup. He had to keep it together. He had to keep it in.

He forced his brain to recall the day that had to be the lowest point of his life. Six years earlier he had stood at the altar in a stiff penguin suit with friends and family watching. He'd been burning with a jealous rage, but kept that stupid fake smile plastered across his mug. He'd handed that shiny diamond ring over to Bill and watched him slide it over Tessa's finger. He'd watched her slip away from him while standing there like an impotent, useless man. Why, why, why had Bill chosen her?

Wade drove the shovel's blade into the dirt and threw the soil over his shoulder. He was pissed, attacking the ground with adrenaline and fury. That asshole of a best friend took the one thing he'd ever wanted. Tessa. Took her because he could. She was weak and vulnerable after their breakup. But it was temporary. Wade didn't blame her, but he blamed him. Bill had violated the first rule of the bro code, not him. Fuck Bill. He was a liar and a hypocrite.

He was about two feet deep, halfway there, when the shovel hit something hard, like a rock. The sound of metal hitting metal was deafening, and Wade swore he saw a spark from the contact. Where the hell had that rock come from? Then he realized it was Bill's rifle barrel. That Remington was definitely useless now.

When he tried to dig again, something felt wrong. Wade held the shovel up towards the sky. In the darkness he could make out a forty-five-degree angle bend in the aluminum blade.

"No, no, no."

He was so close. So close to the keys. So close to warmth, food, and a life with Tessa. He stepped out of the hole, put his foot on the back of the blade and pulled up. Nothing happened. He'd have to give it more torque. He counted to three and jerked up, hard and fast. He heard the snap and fell into the hole, still holding the handle. What the . . . But he knew. The hinges had snapped off from his pull, and now the collapsible shovel with a bent blade was broken in half.

Wade let out a dry, hoarse yell and pounded on the ground. Why? Why this rotten luck? Bill was just two feet away. Then a thought flashed through Wade's mind. Had Bill done this somehow? Even in death he'd probably still be a troublemaking son of a bitch.

Wade began digging with his hands. Clawing and scooping the ground, tossing the dirt behind him as fast he could. Why had he dug so damn deep?

Everything hurt, and nothing made sense anymore. He just needed to do one thing, dig to Bill and get those fucking keys back.

"Come on buddy, you can do it. Dig, dig, dig, dig," Bill's voice shouted in the distance.

Wade stopped for a split second and then went back to scooping and tossing.

"Shut the hell up," Wade responded in a dry, raspy voice.

"Come on, son, can't you do better than that?"

Wade grabbed the blade and started shoveling, one gloved hand on the broken pole and the other underneath the bent spade for support.

"Go Wade, go. Go Wade, go. Woowee, you can do it, boy."

Wade kept at it. Building up a sweat in spite of the freezing air. Then he felt something solid, but not rock solid. Pulling off his gloves Wade felt something like denim and what he suspected to be a shinbone.

"Congrats, man. You found me, but I didn't put your keys in my socks, that's for sure," Bill's voice said with a laugh.

Wade realized that he'd need to dig another two feet out and four deep to get to Bill's waist. Either his pants or jacket pocket, whichever one Bill had stored the keys in. Wade was exhausted, plain and simple. But he knew he had enough energy to dig to those keys. Just enough. And when he got those keys, he'd walk back to the truck, going the right way this time, get inside the truck, turn on the engine to warm up and chow down an extra pack of jerky on the console. Then, when he was ready, he'd go home and take a steaming hot bath to warm up the center of his bones. It would be great if Tessa was there with him too. Maybe she might come over.

"Ain't no way Tessa's gonna take a bath with your dirty ass," Bill said with that idiot laugh.

Was the voice coming from woods or somewhere deep inside of his head? Wade couldn't tell.

"I didn't say nothin'," Wade said as Bill kept laughing.

"Now let me get this straight, bro. You think you're gonna just prance on out of here once you get them keys. Right?"

"Damn straight."

"You don't think you'll succumb to the elements first? You got no water, no food, just sheer exhaustion in zero-degree weather. Hell, man, I'm betting you've got a date with the devil tonight, not Tessa."

Anger surged through Wade, and he started digging like a madman, mumbling, "I'll show you" over and over again as he shoveled soil over his shoulder.

At some point, Wade lost track of time. But he had moved enough earth to get up to Bill's waistline. He felt a lump in Bill's front jeans pocket. He tried to reach inside those tight Wranglers, but the angle was off. He couldn't get his fingers inside. It chilled Wade to feel how cold his friend's corpse was. He pulled out his gutting knife and cut a hole above the keys, cutting into the flesh a little. Bill had been silent through much of the second digging, thank God. Wade tore the pocket lining free and jangled keys in front of Bill's dirt-covered torso.

"See this, bro. I'm gonna make it home tonight. And

once I clean up, I'm gonna bang your wife all night long," Wade shouted hoarsely.

"Look at them keys, Einstein," Bill's voice said in a calm, even tone.

Trembling, Wade held the keys up to the sky where, through the canopy of tree branches, he could make out the Ford logo on the leather keychain. It wasn't his Chevy insignia.

Bill's voice began to chuckle. "Try again, cupcake."

Wade collapsed into ball, huddled around Bill's waist. He had nothing left, zero. But he knew if he fell asleep he would never wake again. He might've even cried if Bill weren't there watching, ready to mock him.

"Come on, you pussy. I'd expect cryin' and whimperin' from most men, but not you, Wade. Not in a million years. You ain't one to ever give up, are ya? Besides, whatcha doing so close to my junk? You aren't gonna blow me, are you, bro?"

With quivering hands, Wade pushed himself up and took the broken spade. He shoved it into the soil and then flung a small amount behind him.

"That's it, buddy. Keep on diggin'."

Wade shook his head and kept shoveling, slowly building momentum. He had to get to the jacket now and check those pockets. One of the sixteen or so that were stitched into hunting jackets these days. He scraped and tossed dirt, his knees straddling Bill's waist "cowgirl style," as the dead man said.

As Wade worked his way up the torso, he stopped to check pockets. He found bullets, tissues, receipts, and, best of all, a half-eaten Snickers bar. Wade consumed the candy bar like a lone coyote scarfing up an injured rabbit. The corn syrup surged to Wade's head. With a burst of energy, he scraped away the dirt wall, finally making it to Bill's chest. Only the ugly bastard's face remained buried.

"Look at you, son," Bill's voice said. "You made it! Like I've always said, nobody can stop Wade once he puts his mind to it."

Wade took off his gloves and searched for Bill's breast pockets. His fingers ran across Bill's sticky bullet hole. Wade's stomach heaved, but he held back the juices inside that hollow cavity. Then he touched a lump. Reaching inside the top pocket, he pulled a set of keys out. They were his. He knew it.

"Well, don't just sit there lookin' at 'em. Get while you still can."

"Yeah," Wade said, or at least he thought he did. "Thanks, buddy."

Wade reached up, setting the keys on top of the hole. He counted to three and stood, barely. He had to use both sides of the pit wall to hold himself up. His entire body quaked as his muscles strained not only to stand, but to function. He needed pull himself out of the grave. He could do it. He knew he could. But when Wade lifted his right leg, the left gave out. He collapsed on top of Bill's hard, uneven corpse. Wade breathed, sucking in the cold air. He listened to the wind pushing the leafless branches overhead.

"Bill," Wade croaked as he shoved the dead man's knee. "Hey, Bill."

There was only silence. Wade tried to stand again, exerting as much energy as he ever had. But nothing happened except inert, useless strain. Exhaustion, entire and complete, enveloped Wade. He fought to keep his eyes open, but they were closing on their own. Automatic shutdown.

"Bill, where are you?" Wade thought. He needed him bad. Needed his best friend's support to get him out of this hole: the fucking hole that he'd dug himself. "You gotta help me out, bro."

Except for the arctic breeze pushing through the naked trees, it was a silent winter night. A feeling of horror overcame Wade as he realized Bill was nothing more than a dead body, and had been ever since he'd shot him earlier in the day. Fading into a deep, eternal sleep, Wade heard Bill's voice one last time.

"See ya in hell, bro."

Here's to Bad Decisions:
Red's Longneck Hooch

HERE'S TO BAD decisions that come with rotten times. If things are going from bad to worse, going to hell in a handbasket at Mach speed like a downhill semi without brakes, and it doesn't look like there's a damn thing you can do about it, you always got one option. Just crack open a bottle of ice-cold Red's Longneck Hooch and pour it down the hatch. This refreshing, mind-numbing concoction is just what you need.

Listening to your wife go on and on about the bills and your lack of steady income? It's time for some Red's Longneck Hooch.

Putting up with the boss man chewing you out for showing up late to work and looking like death warmed over? It's time for some Red's Longneck Hooch.

Noticing the dude with a mullet and muscle shirt who is mad-dogging you from across the bar like you might've pissed on his lawn or knocked up his sister? (Could be both.) It's time for some Red's Longneck Hooch.

Begging your wife for forgiveness after you slapped her for having the gall to say that you've been drinking too much? It's time for some Red's Longneck Hooch.

Restraining your anger with all your might when that pencil-neck boss man gives you his final warning for showing up late? It's time for some Red's Longneck Hooch.

Seeing that cocky mullet-wearing dogface jackass mad-dogging you again at the bar and knowing you got to do something about it soon? It's time for some Red's Longneck Hooch.

Getting pulled over by that son-of-a-bitch highway patrol whose salary you pay with your hard-earned tax dollars, and that mustached fucker has the nerve to give you your second DUI and suspend your damn license? It's time for some Red's Longneck Hooch.

Finding yourself locked out of your double-wide by your wife 'cause you screwed up again, and you're not sure if it's just the DUI or maybe something else? It's time for some Red's Longneck Hooch.

Going over to the trailer that belongs to Darlene (your honey on the side), only to find that mullet-wearing fool smoking outside her door? It's time for some Red's Longneck Hooch.

Sleeping in your wife's car because your truck has been impounded and that bitch still won't let you inside your own damn home? It's time for some Red's Longneck Hooch.

Punching out the boss man after he fires you for being late and unshowered for the hundredth time? It's time for some Red's Longneck Hooch.

Cracking a bottle over the mullet man's head and taking a few good swings before he kicks the living shit out of you? It's time for some Red's Longneck Hooch.

Breaking into your brother-in-law's house so you can steal a couple of the guns he keeps under his bed? It's time for some Red's Longneck Hooch.

Blasting buckshot into the belly of Mullet Man after he answers Darlene's door? It's time for some Red's Longneck Hooch.

Not being able to pull the trigger on Darlene as she pleads for her life and that of your unborn child? It's time for some Red's Longneck Hooch.

Taking cover behind a pecan tree after your wife starts shooting at you from the kitchen window with your own Winchester deer rifle? It's time for some Red's Longneck Hooch.

Speeding down the road after taking a couple of worthless shots at your double-wide you bought with your own hard-earned money only to have the sheriff and highway patrol on your ass? (And you wish like hell you were driving your Ram truck, instead of your wife's puny Hyundai Accent?) It's time for some Red's Longneck Hooch.

Shooting your brother-in-law's Ruger P90 at the law while taking sips of Red's Longneck Hooch and rolling over the spikes spread across the highway causing your wife's Hyundai to careen off the road and tumble down an embankment? It's time for some more Red's Longneck Hooch.

Broken in so many places with pain so intense that nothing makes sense as flames engulf your wife's car? It's too late for Red's Longneck Hooch.

Getting the Yes

JED KNEW WHERE the cameras were. As soon as the old man left the convenience store, he was going in. He waited in his idling truck as the senior citizen jawed with the cashier. Probably this geezer's big social event for the week. At last he lumbered out, but then stopped outside the door and began scratching off lottery tickets with a coin. It looked like he had a stack of them.

"Good Lord Almighty," Jed muttered.

While the old-timer scraped away, a farmer and a plumber both went inside and left with thirty-two-ounce pops. Finally the old man shuffled away, throwing all the cards in the trash and shaking his head in disgust.

Jed checked the road once more and then pulled the hood over his head. He walked in as an Indian kid—way over there India—looked up from a *Car & Driver* magazine. Before the clerk could smile, Jed shoved a .38 Smith & Wesson in his face. Jed kept his head down and away from the camera, which made eye contact difficult.

"Gimme all your money from the register. And put it in a bag. Now."

The teenager shook, but he opened the register and dropped the bills into a paper bag. It didn't look like much.

"Is that all you got?"

"Yes, sir. We are a small mom-and-dad franchise. Unless you want the coins too."

"Naw, that's okay." Jed's brain raced. He needed a lot more. "Do you have a safe?"

"We do, but unfortunately I do not have access to the combination."

Jed nodded. The kid seemed honest enough. He was considering what to do next when a truck pulled up. He grabbed the paper sack of bills and hit the door. Outside he passed a guy with boots and a cowboy hat wearing a sidearm on his belt. Jed made sure to keep his head down and, after a couple of steps, hauled ass to his Ranger.

After speeding down the rural roads and zig-zagging toward home, he decided to pull over and count the money. He counted twice and then a third time. Only one hundred and thirty-seven dollars. Not even close to what he needed. He had to go bigger.

Jed drove to a bank two towns over. It stood out like an island in an asphalt-parking-lot ocean with the continent of Super Walmart on the horizon. People were coming and going inside the bank, so whipping out his revolver wouldn't really work. He'd have to do what most bank robbers do in busy financial institutions.

Waiting in line, he thumbed the hammer back on the .38 inside his hoodie's center pocket and then released it slowly. Trying to calm his nerves. He had to remind himself to keep his head down so the cameras wouldn't capture his face.

"Sir, I'm open."

Jed walked over to the counter where a plump woman with big permed hair bore an ear-to-ear smile.

"Are you depositing or withdrawing?"

"Withdrawing, ma'am."

"Please swipe your card. Did you fill out a withdrawal slip?"

Jed pulled out his bankcard, but stopped himself before swiping it.

"Could I have a slip, please? I forgot to fill one out."

Part of Jed wanted to run. Just go to another bank. But when she slid the slip of paper to him, he knew he had to go through with it.

He scrawled out in block letters: THIS IS ROBERY. GIVE ME ALL UR MONEY OR ILL SHOOT.

Jed pushed the paper back to the woman, feeling sick in his stomach. She looked at the paper for a couple of moments, as if trying to decipher what he had written. Then the color of her skin turned pale as her lips creased from a smile to a frown.

"Sorry ma'am, but if you could give me everything you got in that register," Jed said, trying to keep his voice low and steady. "I'll be on my way."

The woman trembled something fierce. She opened the drawer and started pulling out ones, fives, tens, and twenties. Jed felt his heart rise. This was real money.

"Do you have any hundreds?" Jed asked.

"Not at my drawer. I'd . . . I'd have to ask a colleague."

"No, don't do that. I'll just take what's there. In a bag, please."

"I don't have a bag at my station—"

"Just . . . give 'em to me," Jed said, scooping up the bills and shoving them into the hoodie's center pocket. A few bills hit the ground, but Jed knew he had already taken too long.

"Excuse me, sir. You dropped some money," somebody shouted, but Jed was making a beeline to the door and not turning back.

He counted twice. He had scored only $768 from the bank. It seemed like so much more. With both robberies totaled, he was still under a grand. Jed shook his head. He sat across from the Zales diamond store. He exhaled. He had to do this right. He stepped out of the truck and walked to the front door.

* * *

JED OPENED THE box and took a knee as he choked out the words: "Will you . . . Darla?"

Darla's eyes widened as her jaw dropped. She took the box out of his hand and examined it. Zales was printed on the inside and outside of the box. Plain as day. He remembered she'd said it was the only place to buy a classy diamond. Then she held the ring up to the sun, inspecting the diamond for clarity, he supposed. She twitched her eyebrows. Something she did when calculating math problems.

"Darla?" Jed asked, still on one knee. She looked down at him, surprised, as if he had stepped into the women's restroom to say hello.

"Sorry, Jed. What was that?"

"Will ya marry me? I ain't got much now, and the job don't pay—"

Darla cut him off by holding up her hand and giving him a soft smile that hinted sadness from the corners of her mouth. "Jed, it's not that I don't want to, but . . ."

"Is it Ryan?" Jed said, rising with his fists clenched. That fucker had always had his eye on her.

"Heavens, no. It's just the ring . . ."

"What about it? It's Zales. Cost over a thousand dollars, sugar." Jed felt his heart constricting, his world going just a little woozy. This couldn't happen. Not with what he'd been through to get that dammed thing.

Darla evaluated the ring again. Jed wondered if he should have stuck the receipt in the box. He held his breath as she seemed to appreciate it more. If she'd just say yes and put it on her fluorescent-pink manicured finger. He willed her to do it. Finally, she closed her eyes with forced determination and handed the box back to Jed.

"I just . . . I've always wanted a princess-cut diamond . . . and I want it to be a carat . . . at least. It would be nice if the stone was surrounded by diamonds too. They call it a halo."

Jed felt like he might puke. Of course he should have seen this coming. Nothing was easy with her. At least he hadn't killed anybody to get the money.

"Sorry, Jed, but I know I'm worth it." Darla stepped forward and kissed him on the forehead.

As she walked away, her peroxide ponytail swaying in sync with her Daisy-Dukes-clad ass, Jed bit his lower lip.

He wasn't going to cry. Hell no.

* * *

JED WENT TO Zales the next day and found a ring Darla would love. He'd asked her to come with him, but she'd said, "Surprise me." The problem was that it cost three thousand. Even with the trade-in, he was short two grand.

He knew he couldn't risk it again. Robbing a gas station and a bank in the same day made the news. A punk wearing a hoodie and sunglasses, and carrying a pistol. That was all the cops had, but anybody within a hundred-mile radius who owned a cash register would be ready, fingers twitching on a trigger whenever anyone who looked peculiar walked into their establishment. Besides, both robberies had netted disappointing returns. He even had to throw in some of his own money to buy that ring. He needed a different plan, and then it struck him.

He knew a place where he could find the highest-quality rings for nothing and out in the open. He jumped into his Ranger and drove two hours to downtown St. Louis on a mission.

Sitting in the infield seats, he couldn't believe how close he was to home plate. He'd only seen the game from the bleachers and upper balconies, but using cash from the ring refund afforded him the view he'd dreamed of. He could have experienced all the nuances of the game: the pitcher's grimace hurling a fastball, the popping sound of the ball slamming into the catcher's thick leather mitt, the fine mist of brown dust kicked up from the cleats of the batter inside the box, the grunt of the next batter in the on-deck circle warming up and swinging his weighted bat. He could have noticed all of this and more, but he wasn't watching his beloved Cardinals competing against the visiting Pirates. He kept his eyes on the trophy wives of Northeast Missouri's elite.

Most of the women were blonde, wearing something red and a gallon of make-up. Jed scanned the crowds, looking at manicured left hands and then whether there were children with them or not. He finally picked his favorite. A MILF probably in her mid-forties with a huge rock, a one-point-five or maybe even a two-carat princess cut, with smaller diamonds surrounding it. Her husband looked like a banker with neatly trimmed gray hair, a polo shirt, pleat shorts, and a pair of glasses that cost more than Jed's truck. Jed knew he could take the paper pusher down easily.

Jed tried to enjoy the rest of the game, but he couldn't. He kept looking over his shoulder, making sure the rich couple didn't head out early. That would be just his luck. He might actually enjoy the game from this amazing vantage point, only to lose Darla's perfect engagement ring.

He also had to turn off his cell phone since Darla kept texting nonstop throughout the game. She wanted to know if he'd gotten her ring yet. He'd replied *soon* and *latter 2day*, but it wasn't good enough. She wanted details, and it was starting to piss him off. Jed didn't want to be in that kind of mood, not when he was on a mission of love or something like that. So he finally hit the off button and focused on the couple, who, as far as he could tell, didn't seem to care for each other too much.

When the game was over, a one-zip Cardinal loss on a wild pitch, he followed them past the general parking lot and into a nearby parking garage. Jed really couldn't understand their unhappiness when they walked up to a brand-spanking-new Lexus—what in the world could they be grumpy about? They had everything money could buy. He felt a surge of anger. Ungrateful rich bastards.

Pulling up his hoodie, Jed picked up speed, covering the distance between them. As soon as the man reached for the car door, Jed body-slammed the man against the car. He heard the wind go out of the older man. On the other side of the Lexus, the woman gasped in horror.

"Gimme all of your jewelry, or I'll shoot your husband," Jed said through clenched teeth, trying give his most threatening voice.

He shoved a souvenir bat against the trembling man's back like a gun. He was so close, nobody could tell what he was holding. The woman just stood there looking stupid.

"Do it, Charlene!" the man said to his wife.

She hesitated again, furrowing her brow. Families walked nearby, but they were in their own bubbles, oblivious to the robbery in progress only a few yards away. Jed wished he could have brought his .38 so he could shoot the dumb bitch. She was taking too effing long. But he hadn't been sure if security would let him into the game carrying a concealed weapon.

"I'll do it, lady. I'll kill 'im. I mean it."

Charlene exhaled and rolled her eyes, placing the engagement ring as well as a few other rings and a ladies' Rolex on the roof of the car. For a flash of a second it seemed to Jed that she looked a lot like an older version of Darla if she had money. It felt like a déjà-vu glimpse into the future. Jed shook the thought from his mind. He needed to get rolling.

When he reached up for the jewelry, the scrawny man elbowed him in the gut. Jed brought the mini-bat down on his head. He swiped his hand across the roof as Charlene shot pepper spray across the roof into his face.

Jed ran. He had a handful of something, but he couldn't see anything. He ricocheted off cars and bumped into people, his lungs on fire. He heard the woman shouting behind him and several other voices. A few steps later, he tumbled down a flight of concrete stairs, head over kneecap, crashing deeper into the parking garage. With stinging, blurry sight and every body part screaming pain, Jed searched for an escape until he found a dumpster. Opening the lid, he heaved his banged-up body inside, burying himself deep under dozens of plastic bags full of garbage. One broke, spilling rotten food all over him. He gagged, wanting to leap out screaming and run to the nearest shower and scrub away the nasty filth. But he kept quiet, telling himself to exercise a little bit of self-control. A problem he'd had his entire childhood. He could do it. He'd have to wait it out, because this was bigger than him. This was about Darla, about making her his wife and him her man.

Police walked by with their radios squawking. They even lifted the lid on the dumpster and shone a light around inside, but they didn't dig. Jed couldn't blame them either. It reeked to high heaven.

Jed tried to picture himself in the future with his arm around Darla and a big house with kids and a dog running around. He tried hard, willing it happen in his mind. But he couldn't. All he could envision was living in the stench of now and the time immediately following that, the nearly now. That moment when he knelt on his knee and slipped the damned ring on Darla's finger, waiting for her answer. After that, he had nothing. He didn't know if she'd say yes. If she didn't, he had no idea what he'd do. Probably run head first into a brick wall and hope his head was softer.

Please, God, he prayed. *I know I'm a sinner and not worth your time. But please make Darla say yes. If she does, I'd be mighty grateful. Might even be willin' to take some punishment for a couple of crimes.*

Later, after he was certain the police had left, Jed pushed himself up from the bags and slimy funk. He threw open the lid and inhaled the fresher air of the damp basement garage. It was empty.

Stumbling to the parking lot on a twisted ankle, he made it to his truck sitting alone under a streetlamp. He took off his stinking hoodie and put the ring in his hand. It sparkled something gorgeous under the light. A smile rose from his mouth. But then, looking closer, he noticed his stained hand. It looked like blood. Jed shoved the ring into his Wranglers and started wiping his hand furiously on his hoodie. No, it couldn't be, he told himself. It had to be ketchup or some other gunk. Had to be.

He drove home blasting the radio loud. Country or rock, it didn't matter. He just wanted voices singing and guitars wailing. If an advertisement came on hawking cars or Pepsi or freaking engagement rings, he felt the urge to smash the radio. It was these people, these assholes, who made the world so fucking difficult. He wanted to go back to a time when things were simple. When you were happy being poor and a ring made out of tin was as good as one made of gold. It was the thought, the essence of love, that mattered the most. Not halos, carats, or any of that crap. Just fucking love.

* * *

JED WAS SURPRISED to find Darla waiting outside his duplex. It was after one in the morning.

"I've been texting an' callin' you for the past five hours. Where the hell you've been all night?" She planted her hands on her hips and screwed up her beautiful face so tight it became ugly.

Jed stood by his truck, speechless. He wasn't ready for this. He wanted to shower, put on fresh clothes, and drink a beer. Several of them.

"So?" Darla said, sauntering up to him. A smile started emerging from that rigid scowl. "Did you get me something special today?"

Jed felt in his pockets for it. Panic shot through his body. Maybe that idiot ring fell out in the parking lot when he was trying to wipe his hands off.

Darla stopped a foot away from him and crinkled her nose. "You smell somethin' awful, baby."

Jed felt relief when he found it in his fifth pocket. He pulled out the ring, holding it between his thumb and forefinger. Darla's eyes lit up. Sparkling light danced off the diamonds from the streetlamp overhead. He was about to get on one knee and ask her all over again, when she snatched it from him like a starving dog grabs a bone. She slipped it over her knuckle, admired it on her hand for a couple of seconds, and then squealed.

"It fits! It's perfect. Yes, I'll marry you, Jedediah Crowe." She held out her arms like she wanted to hug or smooch, but then backed off. "Sorry, Jed. I would, but you just stink too much."

Jed beamed as relief flooded over him. The journey was over. Like some fairy tale where the dude had to procure some magical object to win the affection of a princess, he had won Darla. She would become his wife, and they would do that happily ever after thing. However it goes. That thought was wiped away a moment later when two sheriff cruisers screeched to a stop behind his truck. A searchlight blinded him.

Jed froze, unable to move. Which one was it? The gas station, the bank, or Busch Stadium?

"Honey, what's the law doin' here?" Darla asked.

Two deputies jumped out of their cars with their guns pointed at him. No use in running now. Jed smiled, raising his hands in the air. It didn't matter anymore. He'd got what he wanted. Darla had said yes.

A Damn Good Dad

HOW LONG HAS he been up, thirty-two, thirty-five hours? Don't know, and it don't matter. He has been making batches of primo meth, and the product is goooood. He will testify to that. Sampling a little here and there, for quality control, of course. He's always been a good cooker, but this is something special, an intense blast-your-brain-to-the-moon-and-back supreme awesomeness. He has a reason to be cooking. There's always a reason—dough, mullah, greenbacks—but this time it is important. It isn't for him. It's for somebody. Who is it again?

He hears a movement from behind him and twists quickly to see Jenny, Jenny-Penny-oh-so-skinny, waking up. Her sleepy, soft blue eyes look at him. He guesses she's smiling, but can't tell because she wears that paper mask that doctors wear, except hers has jagged hand-drawn vampire fangs and red Magic Marker blood dripping off of them.

See, I'm a good father, a damn good dad, he thinks. Not like Clyde McDonnell, tweaked out of his fucking gourd, who put his newborn in a freezer. Or Jimmy Treat who left his toddler in a car for three days in ninety-degree heat. Or even worse that asshole Steve Hobbes who sold his daughter to pervs so he could buy more crank. Not me, no way, no sir, no how. I've got her with me so no harm will come and she is protected. I'm the best father in Okfuskee County. Other tweakers might—

"Daddy?" Jenny-Penny asks.

"Yes, honey-bunny?"

"When's Mommy coming back?"

He stops, holding a beaker full of steaming anhydrous ammonia. That's the reason for this meth-rage cooking spree. Bail money for Gloria.

"Well funny-bunny, I gotta get this batch here done and maybe one more. Then we sell it to Uncle Blaine and then we get Mommy out in no time flat."

"Are you making metha . . . methafetamins?"

"Oh no, honey, this is . . . medicine for sick folks." See, he's protecting her from illegal activities.

She sits up. "Wha's in it?"

"Well, a little of this, pseudoephedrine, and a little of that, sodium, and then mix it with ammonia and let it boil an' bubble while adding just the right amount of etha-nol . . . without exploding, and when the ammonia evaporates, we get these beautiful, sparkly crystals of meth . . . medicine."

"Suuudo . . . sudodoctorine?"

Losing his concentration, he looks over at her. What did she say? That mask is creeping him out. It looks like the blood is dripping off the mask on the floor. Those teeth chomping. He looks back at his chemistry project. What is he mixing again? He looks at the small kitchen crammed into this camping trailer. His lab. See, he keeps the chemicals out of the house next door. That way every-body's safe. What a good man. No, a good dad.

"Daddy?"

He feels a tug on his pants and looks down to see a three-foot-something creature with hungry fangs. He shouts and jumps back, tripping over a boot, and tosses the flask of whatever he was holding. A flame shoots up from the kitchen sink, and the ceiling is engulfed in orange heat. The little creature screams a high-pitched squeal.

Oh shit, oh shit. Fire. I've got to save 'em. He turns, grabbing the tray of drying meth crystals off the dining table and hits the front door. It won't open. He reaches for the door handle, the tray tilts, and a few crystals fall. NOOO! The fire is intense and he feels flames licking his neck and ears. He opens the door, telling himself he'll come back later for them, and sprints into the open air.

An explosion blasts him to his knees into the hard dirt, but he holds the tray steady. Only a few crystals fell. He smiles, setting the tray down and arranging the crystals in precise order. He thinks, I'm a good cook. I take good care of my product. I'm the best damn . . . Then he realizes.

"Jenny, Jenny-Penny!"

Panicked, he scans the yard but doesn't see her. The camper is aflame, the roof totally blown off. No, no, no. He's a good father, a damn good dad. Nothing bad can happen to Jenny. He runs to the door, and the handle singes his hand, but he tugs and is engulfed by an ocean of flames.

Tim's Mommy Lied

HELLO, MY NAME is Tim. Even though I'm short, I am almost seven years old. I used to live in a small house not too long ago. Then the lights stopped working. I couldn't watch TV, and that made me sad. That made Mommy sad too, but probably more angry than sad. She yelled at Daddy, wanting to know what he was gonna do about it.

Daddy yelled back at Mommy. So I went to my room to hide under the bed. Sometimes they throw things. Sometimes they hit each other. I didn't want to get hit.

Then I heard Daddy slam the door and drive the car away. I crawled out from under the bed. I saw Mommy crying. She picked up a glass straw and lighted a small fire under it to make herself feel better. Mommy breathed the stinky smoke in the straw.

I remember playing with Pete for a while in the dark. He's my Teddy Bear. Pete has one eye. When Mommy bought him for me, one eye was starting to come out. Then it fell out, and I lost it. I feel bad for Pete. He can only see half of the world.

Later on I heard Daddy's car outside. He came inside and waked up Mommy. He walked like he breathed a bunch of smoke from a glass straw. His hands were on his belly. There was a dark spot there. Dark stuff was on his hands too.

Daddy said, "We gotta go."

Mommy asked, "What happened?"

"We gotta go," he said again. Then he walked out the door.

Me and Mommy walked to the car. It was cold and

dark outside. When I got inside the car, I saw a bag in the backseat. The bag had red sticky goo on it like Daddy's belly. I put Pete next to the bag.

Daddy drove out of town, but the car kept moving back and forth. He couldn't keep the car straight. I remember squeezing Pete hard to keep him safe. Mommy told Daddy he needed to go to the doctor.

He said, "No. We gotta get out of town."

Then he fell asleep. The car went all crazy, going off the road. I remember bouncing in the seat, almost hitting my head on the roof. Mommy stopped the car on the grass. She shook Daddy and screamed his name real loud. Then she stopped doing that and cried real hard.

I asked, "What's wrong with Daddy?"

She said, "Daddy's dead."

I helped Mommy take Daddy out of the car. Daddy's foot was really heavy. There was a big bright moon making everything spooky white. I could see my breath in the air. Mommy's too. But not Daddy's. Even though his eyes were open, Daddy was dead.

We put Daddy under a tree and then found a bunch of sticks and leaves to put on top of him. We kept putting more and more on top him until we couldn't see Daddy no more.

Then Mommy cried. I guess I cried too. A little.

Mommy asked Daddy, "What are we going to do now?" Which is kind of silly since he was dead and under all of those sticks and leaves.

Then I told Mommy about the bag with the sticky goo in the car. I had to run to keep up with Mommy because she walked super fast. When she opened the bag we saw a bunch of small clear plastic bags of white stuff that Mommy smoked in her glass straw. There was money inside the bag too. A lot of it. Red-black sticky stuff was on some of them.

Mommy smiled. It was the biggest smile I've seen her have.

She said, "Everything's gonna be OK, Tim. Everything's going to be wonderful."

I'm not sure if she was lying or not. We've been in this motel for a few days. Mommy went to the bathroom yesterday and locked the door. She hasn't come out no matter how hard I knock. I peed in the trash can and bought a Pepsi from the machine, but I'm pretty hungry. At least I get to watch TV. That's OK, but not wonderful.

Maybelle's Last Stand

MAYBELLE EASES BACK and forth in her rocking chair, slow but steady, on the front porch of her single-room abode. Keeping her cataracted eyes on the dusty road ahead, she rubs her arthritic hands together underneath a quilt, trying to keep her fingers agile. A tall man approaches her shack with the setting sun behind his back, silhouetting him. She's not sure who it is, but he's white by his swagger and definitely the law because of the gun hanging off the belt on his hip. When he finally reaches the porch, propping his boot on the first step, she can tell it is the devil himself, Sheriff Reed.

Maybelle prays, hoping that her grandson is quiet now. No need to agitate a cowardly lawman. The sheriff takes his hat off, wiping away beads of sweat.

"Howdy, ma'am."

Maybelle nods, but doesn't smile. She doesn't smile for any white man, especially if he's on her land. Smilin' and yessirin' was something her parents did against their will when they were another man's property. This was hard land that she, her parents, her brothers and sisters, her husband, and her children toiled over to make a living.

"I'm looking for your grandson, Ernest Young." The lawman wouldn't meet her eyes.

"Ain't around here."

The lawman chuckles as if he is dealing with a half-witted child. "That ain't gonna fly. You're gonna let me look around here. I don't need to be askin', I'm just tryin' to be polite."

"What is it that you want Ernest for?"

The sheriff turns and spits on the cracked earth. "We got another dead girl. A white girl. She was raped and then strangled to death."

Maybelle scoffs and shakes her head. "That's a cryin' shame."

"Yes, it is. And I don't see nothin' funny about it."

"She'd be the fourth one now, right, Sheriff? And yet three good men have been hung."

"They ain't good. None of 'em. They're rapists and murderers"

"Every one of them?" The lawman wouldn't meet her eyes. "I suspect it's a white man."

"Impossible," he says too quickly.

"You know, I think you've got a little strategy goin' on here, Sherriff."

"I don't care to hear any of your theories right now."

"Seems the land of three negroes, rightfully given to them by the United States is bein' taken. Amassed, you might say."

"Now you best watch your—"

"And sweet little girls seem to be dyin' every couple of months. So I'm wonderin' which is it you like more, Sheriff? The flesh of innocent young girls or land?"

The sheriff's nostrils flare, but fear widens his eyes. "You ain't to talk to me that way. I'm gonna teach you some manners, nigger bitch."

He yanks the pistol from his holster. Maybelle's quilt explodes from under her. Her body rocks back in the chair from the blast. The sheriff drops his gun, having brought it only halfway up. He looks at the burning hole in the quilt and then down to his stomach. His potbelly pulses out crimson goop.

Maybelle pushes the quilt onto the splintered porch and stomps out the flame. She puts the heavy, old Colt Peacemaker in her left hand. Shaking her right fingers, she feels like she might've fractured something.

"Kick like the dickens, don't ya," she mutters to the

gun.

With both hands, she points the gun at the sheriff's head. Blood oozes between his fingers from the hole in his belly, dripping into a red pool next to his pistol on the porch steps. Maybelle thinks his face is almost as white as the sheets he and his kind put over their heads some nights when they get the spirit of the devil in them.

"Any last words, lawman? I hear you've never had the decency to've asked us coloreds that before you lynch us. But I suppose I'm better than you. A whole lot better."

The sheriff reaches for his gun, but it slips from his bloody fingers.

"They'll kill you, you and your grandson. Hang y'all up by that tree in the front." He gasps, wincing in agony. He glares at her as mean as a dying man can. "You can't shoot a sheriff out here, not in these parts." If he had the strength, he would spit on her porch.

"But it looks like I most certainly did shoot myself a sheriff. See, I've been havin' a dilemma for quite a while now. Either I kill a sheriff, that'd be you," Maybelle says, pointing the unsteady gun at the lawman. "Or let him live and keep killin' white babies. Truly it don't matter 'cause we get hung all the same."

She cocks the hammer back with her left hand. Much harder than it oughta be.

"They'll kill your boy, you know."

"No, they won't. I can guarantee you that."

Holding the pistol with both hands, Maybelle pulls the trigger. Sheriff Reed's brains blast out the back of his head as he falls to the ground. She would've never suspected he'd had so much in that dull, perverted head of his. But maybe it's all putrid meat. Sure smells that way.

More white men would be coming along shortly. And they'd be crazy mad like a bunch of hornets knocked out of their nest. She supposes she has three bullets left, but isn't sure and doesn't even know how to open the noisy contraption to check. She was surprised when the gun fired the first time. It was handed down from her father to her brother and then to her after Willie had been hung. Must've been the Lord's doin' to make such an old device still work. She says a quick prayer of gratitude to God for being there in her time of need.

Yep, them white men will definitely kill me whenever they decide to show, she thinks. At least they'll never get their grubby hands on Ernest. Standing on aching legs, she hobbles from the rocking chair to the door.

"Please, Lord, let me take a couple of 'em to hell with me."

She knows that's where's she's going. No doubt about it.

Opening the front door, she sees her grandson sitting at the table with his bowl of beans. Almost the same way she left him when she went out to the porch. Except the poor boy's face is planted in the bowl. Stone cold dead.

No, sir, Ernest isn't going to be hung, left swinging for days in the sun under the bridge so white kids can disgrace his body. She's seen too much of that awfulness already. Running her callused fingers through his unruly hair, she inhales a quick, shallow breath. Just fourteen years of age, the dear boy. The child was so sweet, so honest and sincere, it broke her heart when she thought about him.

Ernest came running to the house an hour earlier, eyes full of tears and fright. He had the misfortune of seeing the sheriff pick up a little white girl in his car a few days before. When she turned up dead this morning, he told a few folks what he'd seen, only to find out the sheriff was looking for him. Maybelle knew what was in store for her grandson. And she swore to him, invoking the name of Jesus and the Father himself, that she'd keep those white men from harming him.

Sitting the boy upright, Maybelle takes a washcloth and hobbles over to a pail. Dipping the soiled rag into the water, she wrings it out, twisting it back and forth in her gnarled hands. She hates to turn around, to bear witness to the murder she has committed, but she must. Looking at her grandson, she sees the poisonous red beans sticking all over his face.

"Oh good Lord, Ernest. Can't you go anywhere without makin' a mess?" she says in a tone she used on all of her grandbabies. "Let me wash you up. Just hold still now."

With the cloth, she pulls off one bean at a time, dropping them into the bowl. "Now I know you're up there in heaven, Ernest, looking down at me and wonderin' why on earth I'd do such an awful thing to you. The only blood I got left in this world." She exhales and starts washing up his face. "I want you to know it wasn't easy for me to mix the poison into the pot of beans I had boilin', but you see there just wasn't another way. With the sheriff comin' after you and nobody but a decrepit old ninny to defend you . . ."

Maybelle shakes her head, looking into the boy's wide-open, unblinking eyes. "This harsh, evil world wasn't designed for somebody like you. There are too many damnable jagged edges out there that'd rip a soft boy like you to shreds. I've lost too many loved ones to horrors, you see. My brother got hung on the word of a lying white man, your mama died in childbirth, your daddy sliced his arm on rusted plow and no white doctor'd see him until it was too late. No sir, Ernest. You had nowhere to go. Not with an evil lawman like Sheriff Reed on your tail and the demons that'll follow him."

She hears an engine and the crunch of gravel in the distance. This is it. Armageddon on the homestead. Maybelle closes Ernest's eyes and steps back. He looks peaceful in the chair. She prays to God again, but doubts He's listening anymore considering what she did to her grandson. But didn't He sacrifice His own son for a greater cause? Maybe Jesus could intercede for her. She hears voices, white, shouting in horror and disbelief.

"Sheriff Reed's dead. That nigger boy done shot him."

She prays for strength and the ability to kill as many of them as there are bullets left in the old gun. Swinging the door wide open, she sees three men in tan deputy uniforms standing over the dead sheriff. They look up in shock. She raises the pistol and begins firing.

Because

HE STOPPED READING when he was ten because: his pa
said it was a waste of time; he was spanked until welts
appeared on his rear after his pa found a copy of *Charlotte's
Web* hidden under his bed, and his ma was beaten for
secretly buying it for him; real men didn't read.

In middle school he beat up a kid with glasses because:
the nerd made the rest of the class look like dummies by
answering all the questions; the nerd acted all superior; the
nerd read books.

He dropped out of school at fourteen because: it was a
waste of time; his pa needed help in the shop; school was
for pussies anyway.

He stole a car because: he was bored; a fire raged inside, and if he didn't do something crazy, he might hurt
somebody; he wanted to shock his tight-assed friends who
were always in school.

He rammed the stolen car into a police roadblock because: he wasn't pulling over with his buddies in the car
regardless of how many times they pleaded for him to stop;
there was a chance he might break through; why not? The
car wasn't his anyway.

He was tried as an adult for manslaughter because: his
friend Eric flew through the windshield; destroying police
property was not appreciated by prosecutors or tax-paying
jurors; unlike other juvenile delinquents, he couldn't prove
he had a future.

In jail he learned that his pa lost the auto shop because:
fewer people were driving older cars that didn't require
computers to fix up; his pa kept ignoring audit letters from

the IRS; hiring his defense lawyer had drained what was left of the family savings.

Later his pa shot himself and his ma because: his pa blamed her for their wayward son; his pa couldn't stand living every day as a failure; his pa was a selfish asshole.

When was he released from prison at twenty-six, he went back to his old house that his aunt had kept for him but could not sleep the first two nights in his old bed because: the silence was too much without the noises of his cellmate and other prisoners; the silence was too much without the presence of his mother in her house; the silence was too much.

He knew Sadie would be his when he saw her at the bar because: she smoked like a chimney, and he took that mean she was easy; she had trouble, literally, written across her breasts on a tight tank top; she kept gazing at his oversized biceps and prison ink.

He robbed a convenience store because: he needed money; nobody was hiring ex-cons; Sadie got pregnant.

He shot the clerk because: he didn't want a witness; the kid had an attitude; the kid was reading a book.

Cornered in a church parking lot, he shot at the cops because: he didn't want go back to prison; he didn't want to live; he didn't want to be a loser "my-dad's-in-jail" father.

He punched out his attorney because: his public defender negotiated a life sentence; his public defender was probably a rich do-gooder who didn't know what real life was like; he had no other outlet to release his frustration.

In prison, he joined the Aryan Brotherhood because: they offered protection; he understood the group; he got to beat on others with immunity.

Five years later, he started shit out on the basketball court because: he wanted to make a reputation; he was frustrated by the Brotherhood's rigid structure; seeing his daughter Eva earlier that day for only thirty minutes shredded his heart.

He read in isolation because: he was bored out of his skull when he reluctantly opened a mangled copy of *Of Mice And Men*; books offered a whole helluva lot more than any movie he had ever seen; he enjoyed it.

He took a swing at a guard moments after he was released from isolation because: he didn't want to be around ignoramus racists anymore; he wanted to continue reading without being harassed by illiterate idiots; he wanted to write a story for Eva and needed the privacy.

He read fiction over biography and history because: fiction offered limitless opportunities rather than nonfiction's concrete reality; fiction was never finished until the words "the end"; fiction made the world much bigger than the one he was living in.

He took a job at the prison library because: he got access to books when they first came in; he met other like-minded inmates and limited his time with the Brotherhood; he could continue to write stories for his daughter.

He was upset when Sadie published the fairy-tale stories he'd written for Eva because: the stories were meant for his daughter's eyes only; a national controversy exploded around him, debating whether a prisoner should be able to sell a book from jail; the Brotherhood ordered him to stop writing immediately because it made them look soft.

He taught literacy classes to other inmates because: he was tired of being a racist thug; he needed to spread goodwill after all the bad he had created; he felt compelled to do it regardless of the consequences.

When he was betrayed, stabbed fifteen times by a young protégé, he forgave the kid in his dying breaths because: he knew he would have done the same thing as a young man wanting to win favor with the Brotherhood; he had sold enough books to put Eva through college; he knew his legend would grow stronger in death, and there was nothing anybody could do about it.

BRUISED:
STORIES FROM THE WEST

Incident on the 405

JESSICA TAN EASED the Rolls Royce onto the 405 on-ramp from Santa Monica Boulevard and instantly regretted it. Her smartphone had shown yellow, medium traffic, but what she encountered was a barely crawling red. How smart was that?

She looked at the time: 4:42 p.m. She needed to have this polished British export up to Clive Winterborne's mansion on Mulholland by five, or he'd blow up . . . again. That horndog was either making creepy advances at her or pissed off and screaming. It wasn't like it was her fault that Julio, the only person Clive designated to touch his prize possession at Tidal Wave Car Wash, had been on lunch break when she arrived in the Silver Ghost. And now, this gridlock.

Jessica hoped to be the first assistant in years to last more than six months. If she could do that, she could easily find a better job with a reputation as the assistant who managed the devil himself and perhaps cut a path to being a producer. But with only two months to go, she was beginning to doubt if she would last that long.

* * *

SADIE BITTERMAN BIT her lip hard to keep tears out of her eyes. She could taste the blood. Was this the lowest low? The depths kept sinking deeper. Even now, after straightening out her life, it all flew back in her face. Splat. She wasn't a criminal. Not anymore. She was doing her best to keep a job, but this fucking traffic, she'd be late again. And what would she tell Walter, the teenage shift manager? Sorry, Walt, I had to go to court today in

Torrance . . . Child custody . . . No, I didn't win. Thanks for asking. She'd have a lot to talk about at her Narcotics Anonymous meeting on Monday.

She fingered a plastic bag on the passenger seat. Gifts ungiven. A Hulk shirt for Tyler and a pocketknife for Edgar. Security hadn't let her bring the bag inside the court because of the knife. It was small, a two-inch blade at best. How much damage could anybody do with that? She knew the real answer, a lot. She'd seen fellow prisoners sliced with shards of glass or shivs made from broken plastic bottles. But a ten-year-old boy wouldn't know, and didn't they all carry knives? Her brother had. What was the big deal?

Sweat ran down her face; the Oldsmobile's A/C was busted. She was feeling it, the buzz. An urge to pull off this eight-lane parking lot and find Parker. He'd lived in Venice the last time she'd bought from him. The man had the magic powder that made things better, things that methadone could not cure. She inhaled and exhaled. Just make it up to the Valley. NA's motto was "One day at a time," but right now she was taking it one minute at a time.

* * *

"YES, SIR . . . I know. I'm driving as fast as the traffic will let me . . . It's not my fault." Jessica heard her voice crack and hated herself. Clive hung up on her. How could anybody endure this asshole? She hadn't gone to Berkeley for this. Fuck him and his antique show car. It was so ridiculous to drive in America with the steering wheel on the right side. She saw a gap opening to her left and steered the Rolls into it.

* * *

SADIE WAS CHANTING a sobriety mantra when she saw traffic had moved a little. She had just hit the accelerator when a fancy ancient car pulled in front of her. She slammed on the brakes and laid into the horn. Fuck this rich guy. Who did he think he was? Men with their penis extensions, compensating for their inadequacies. Men who prey on the weak, taking advantage of the innocent. She was surprised when a lady's arm reached out of the passenger window with a middle finger pointed straight into the air.

Uh-uh. This was not the day for anybody to fuck with her. She'd already been screwed once today. That know-it-all judge probably collected useless cars, too. He hadn't even listened to her when she pleaded for her kids back. She was off the H. She had a job and was looking for an apartment.

She eased the Olds as close to the Rolls as she could. Just flip me off again, bitch, she thought.

* * *

JESSICA LOOKED IN her rearview mirror. Some crazy white-trash bitch in a clunker was riding her ass. Just what she needed.

It was 4:50. No way she'd make it in time. He'd sent her on a fool's errand. Clive needed a reason to rant and rave. A screamer, they'd warned her. But the production company he ran had had a string of hits until this year: a couple of hundred-million-dollar flops and this latest stinker, premiering tonight, based on the board game Yahtzee. He'd definitely take its failure out on her.

Her phone rang. It was Clive again. As she tapped the talk button on her Bluetooth, the car ahead of her stopped suddenly. Jessica stomped on the brakes and then heard a crash behind her as the Rolls lurched forward.

"Shit!" Jessica screamed.

"What happened?" Clive shouted over the phone.

"I don't know. Somebody rear-ended me."

"What the ... That is a priceless antique. You ... you're fired."

"I didn't hit anybody."

"If you had been here earlier ... I'll make you pay

for—"

Jessica hung up. Great, now she didn't have a job, all because of some idiot.

* * *

SADIE SHOVED THE knife in her back pocket and was out of her car, fists clenched. She ignored the honking cars behind her and focused on the expensive car. She saw the passenger, a small Asian chick, aka the bird flipper, get out and check the rear of it. Where was the driver? Then she saw the steering wheel on the right side. What the hell?

* * *

THE STEEL BUMPER was dented, but the paint on the body was untouched. Jessica sighed. If she hadn't left her own car at Clive's house, she'd just leave the Rolls in the middle of the 405 and walk home. Or maybe catch a bus if she could figure out how that worked. Her phone rang, but she ignored it. Fuck Clive.

The loser woman strode to the front of her piece-of-crap car, hands balled like the bell had rung in a tough-man contest. The Oldsmobile's plastic grill was smashed in and cracked.

"You're going to pay for this," she said to Jessica, hands on her hips, trying to stare her down. She was tall, almost a foot taller than Jessica's five-two.

Jessica noticed small blue tattoos on her hands, and then the coldness of her green eyes. Hard and desperate. Was she a crackhead?

"I hope you have insurance, because you just hit Clive Winterborne's extremely rare and priceless 1924 Silver Ghost, lady," Jessica said.

* * *

SADIE SHOOK. SHE was so screwed. Of course she didn't have insurance. How could she afford it with her minimum wage job? She was still saving up to get first and last month's rent for an apartment. If anything, she should have home insurance since she slept in the car. She felt her hand slide to her back pocket, toward the knife, but stopped herself from pulling it out. Don't give in to impulses. Sally, her sponsor, would be proud.

"You won't believe this," she said. "I got rear-ended by an uninsured crazy bitch."

It took Sadie a second to realize that she wasn't talking to her, but into that annoying earpiece that a-holes wore in the grocery store, looking as if they were having conversations with their multiple personalities. That Asian chick thought she was crazy. Ha, she'd show that bitch what crazy was.

* * *

"IT'S NOT MY fault," Jessica pleaded as she endured a tirade of profanities in her right ear. "What the hell?" she said as she watched the undoubtedly high woman smash the brake light of the Rolls with the heel of her sandal. "Hey, cun—"

* * *

"WHAT HAPPENED?" CLIVE screamed into the phone, but all he heard was a loud grunt. "Jessica, Jessica! What happened? Answer me, you idiot!" Not his Silver Ghost. Why did he trust her or anybody else to drive it? That frigid bitch was so fired.

* * *

IT TOOK JESSICA almost a full minute to answer Clive after she crumpled to her knees, watching the Rolls head up the 405 through the gap their stopped cars had created. She was out of breath because the wind had been knocked out of her when that piece of white trash sucker-punched her and jumped in Clive's car. But looking down, it was worse. She was bleeding. "Clive . . ." she said, with tears welling. She heard static. The phone was in the car, and the Bluetooth signal was getting fainter. "I've been stabbed."

* * *

CLIVE STOOD FUMING in his tuxedo. He looked at his Ulysse Nardin watch. He had hoped to fire that little Chinese twat in person when she finally got her skinny ass up here, but God knew when she'd finally make it now. Even if she had sex with him on his desk, it was too late. You can make some mistakes and get by, but you don't mess with the Silver Ghost.

He didn't need this. Not tonight. But he had prepared for such a disaster and already had a limo waiting. He'd ordered it days earlier without telling Jessica. If she were worth her salary, she would have found a way to get the Ghost to him without a scratch.

He tapped a number on his phone. "This is Clive Winterborne. Have my car here in ten minutes. I'll leave the gate open."

* * *

SADIE DROVE THE Rolls, steering the oversized boat and mashing gears with its weird clutch through traffic toward to the nearest exit. At least her uncle, may he rot in hell, had taught her to drive a stick. She couldn't believe what she'd done. But when that little woman, thinking she was all-superior, called her a crazy bitch, something snapped. She went reptilian, pure instinct. The blade was between her knuckles, the hilt in her palm. Just like a shivved spoon in prison. It happened so quickly that she couldn't stop herself. She was destined for the slammer again.

Maybe that was where she belonged. Her kids might graduate from high school before she got out now. She felt the buzz inside, the urge to get high, but she swallowed the thought. Stay away from Parker. Stay sober.

With a bloody right hand on the wheel, she reached for the glove box with her left. One thing was certain, she couldn't run for long in this weird, old car. Insane rich people putting steering wheels wherever they want. She knew she needed to ditch it, but then what? Hitchhike?

Nobody picked up hitchhikers anymore. She found a garage remote and registration in the glove box. Perhaps she could drive to that bitch's house and take another car. A more modern one. Maybe swipe some jewelry too.

A jolt of panic hit Sadie when she realized that the Highway Patrol would find out who she was in a matter of minutes. Even though her own car wasn't registered to her—she had bought it for $300 cash, no questions asked—there was that legal paperwork forbidding her to visit her sons. It sat wadded in the Oldsmobile's front seat next to the Hulk shirt. Tyler's gift.

"Shit!" she yelled, pounding the steering wheel.

She couldn't do anything right for her boys. But if she were ever going to see them again, she had to get away. Her mind flew, calculating. She needed a different car, some cash, and enough time to make it to Venice, her former stomping grounds. That was old Sadie, the one who had served three years for robbery because her addiction compelled her to get money by any means. She had vowed to stay away from there, from Parker, from her old friends and old, nasty habits.

But that was before today, before five minutes ago. Smack users from her past might take her in and hide her for a while. Maybe she could eventually escape to Mexico and take her kids with her—after she found out where the foster program hid them. She squeezed her eyes shut, knowing this was an addict's hope. Unbelievable, unrealistic. But she had to believe she'd make it out of this mess. She must.

* * *

JESSICA DIDN'T KNOW how or why, but she was behind the wheel of this filthy, smelly Oldsmobile. Of course she was making it even more gunky with her sticky blood on the steering wheel and seat. She knew she should have stayed on the freeway and waved for help or turned the car toward the UCLA hospital. But she was pissed.

The sharp, uninterrupted pain from the stab wound pushed her forward. If an intestine were perforated, toxic fluid might poison her body, but it seemed the blade was not long, probably a pocketknife, and her Pilates-ized ab muscles had taken brunt of the metal. If the knife was as clean as this car . . . She tried to remember when she had her last tetanus shot. She compressed a child-sized Incredible Hulk shirt against the wound. Why do only idiots breed?

She could have made a decent doctor, but one year of med school and too many asshole classmates had made her decide to move to Hollywood instead. Of course, she had jumped from the pot into the fire. And it hadn't been popular with the family, but she had wanted to do things her way. Now, defying logic again, Jessica followed that silver speck of a half-million-dollar automobile in the distance, puttering in traffic at five miles an hour. She would find the woman and bring her to justice.

She watched in surprise as the Rolls took the Skirball exit. Where was this crazy bitch going?

* * *

SADIE TOOK THE exit up Skirball Center Drive toward Mulholland Drive. The registration address was on Mulholland, but she had to make a decision: left or right? As a girl growing up in the San Fernando Valley, she had dreamed of owning a mansion on the famous drive that, to her, gave a total view of the world. Now she had the garage door opener to one of these palaces. She would finally be in one, if only for a moment. Just long enough to grab keys and snatch some valuables. She made a right, heading east. That's where she would want her house to be.

* * *

CLIVE WAS SHOCKED to see the Silver Ghost pull into his circular driveway and head to the garage. Didn't Jessica fill out a report with the Highway Patrol? There had to be an official report so he could file insurance for the damage. He stormed out the front door, eying the back of his beloved car. A yelp escaped his lips in spite of himself. It wasn't bad, not as bad as he had envisioned, but the tail lamp was broken and the metal bumper dented. He was going to give Jessica all holy hell. He ran over to the driver's door and flung it open. He stepped back in shock as a tall, thin woman he had never seen before shot out of the seat and shoved a bloody pocketknife to his throat.

"Make one stupid move, and I'll slice your neck open."

* * *

IT ALMOST MADE Sadie laugh. A grown man in a tuxedo pissing himself, literally. He mumbled words like take anything you want, please, I don't want to die, and all that pathetic sentimental shit. He wasn't going to . . . oh, yes, he was crying. Tears streamed down as fast as his urine.

She guessed this whimpering fool was the little Asian woman's man. He was considerably older, pudgy, and pasty. He probably worked at home making bank in fraudulent investment schemes on the internet. Considering the Mediterranean-style mansion with landscaped gardens—heaven as best as man could build—she knew he made more in an hour than she would make in a year or three.

"Let's go inside," she said through gritted teeth. Hopefully there would be some rope to tie up this blubbering fool. Then she could find another less pretentious car and split.

They started to shuffle up the walkway when she heard another car. She turned to see a stretch limo easing down the drive. She pressed the knife to his stomach.

"Who is that?"

"It's . . . it's my ride."

"Send them . . ." Sadie started to say and then hesitated. "Where is it taking you?"

"Graumann's Chinese Theatre for . . . my premiere."

Sadie calculated as fast as she could. A movie guy, of course. The car came to a stop, and the driver jumped out running to the passenger door. Another witness. But she had never been inside a limo . . . and she had never been to a movie premiere. Just life in crappy apartments, crack houses, and prison. She knew she needed to escape Los Angeles, wait for this fucked-up situation to blow over, and then come back and get her boys. But a voice, that internal demon that seemed to guide her life more than sane logic, asked when had anything nice ever happen to her. Her entire life had been shitty. If anything she could ride in luxury with pissypants to Hollywood and then jack another car there.

"Can you get me into the premiere?"

"Sssure," the movie man said. The lie was transparent, but Sadie was willing to swallow it for the moment.

"Tell the driver to get back in the car. We can close our own door."

* * *

AS JESSICA DROVE to Clive's house, the pain in her belly grew. She saw a limo leaving from his gated drive. Maybe the psycho bitch didn't go to his place. Anyhow, it looked like her boss was going to make it to the premiere on time. She felt a moment of relief, but then confusion. How did he get a limo so quickly? It wasn't like there were fleets with drivers ready to go on a moment's notice on a Thursday.

She put in the code to the gate and was surprised to see the Rolls Royce in the drive. That didn't make any sense at all. Hopefully her phone was still in it. She parked and noticed a crumpled piece of paper on the passenger seat with her blood on it. She opened it. So the psycho wasn't allowed to see her kids. That was a good thing. Jessica was going to take Sadie Bitterman down.

She pushed herself out of the wretched, reeking Olds. Standing felt like fifty knives stabbed her stomach. She walked over to the British import. The door was open. Looking on the seat, she saw her purse turned over, wallet open and stripped of cash. Her phone was on the floor. Jessica reached for it, feeling burning pain. She dialed nine-one, but her finger hovered over the last digit.

She needed medical attention. The yellow Hulk T-shirt had turned red. But things weren't making sense. The limo leaving, the Rolls in the driveway. Was Clive in the house? She wanted to go inside and find out what was happening. She could treat the wound in there. Besides, Clive would hate to have an ambulance drive up to his house with all his neighbors watching. It would be a display of weakness. Although Jessica was short, she was not weak. She would rather die than give her a-hole boss the satisfaction of believing that lie. She pocketed her phone and staggered into the house.

"Hello," she shouted. Deathly silence.

She shuffled over to Clive's office adjacent to the marble-floored living room that was larger that her apartment. He had a restroom in the office and hopefully some hydrogen peroxide. She did not want to go into the creep's bedroom if she could help it.

As she passed his desk toward the bathroom she noticed an envelope with her name on it and hesitated. She needed to clean up. She needed to call the police and an ambulance. But what had he left for her?

She opened it, and her eyes began to water. It all made sense now. She had been set up to fail. She wouldn't have sex with him so he needed an excuse. That lowdown, ungrateful, son of a . . .

* * *

THEY WERE STUCK in traffic inching down Laurel Canyon.

"I can have the best lawyers in the world work with you to get you out of this mess. Plus, I can give you all the money you'd ever want if you just let me go."

He was shaking and sweating, lying his ass off faster than a speed freak. Sadie wished she had a larger knife so that she could cut out his tongue. She felt the buzz again and swallowed the urge to shoot up. She needed to stay focused.

Sitting next to the door in the rear seat, she kept the knife pushed against his flab. The damned thing wouldn't penetrate anything but blubber, it was so small, but that idiot didn't know better. He stank of pee, and she wanted to pour some of the liquor from the wet bar on his lap just to take the edge off. She still hadn't figured a way out yet, and this motormouth was wrecking her concentration.

"Hold it. So you're saying you'd give me a million dollars right now if I let you go," she said.

"Easily."

"You're full of shit."

Before Clive could protest, his phone rang. The ring tone was familiar. Bum-bum-bum. Bum-bum-bum. What was it? Three blind mice, three blind mice. That was it. He started to reach for it, but then looked at his captor for guidance.

"Who is it?" she asked.

"Jessica. My assistant. She was my assistant. It's her ring tone."

"Is she Asian?"

He nodded.

"Give me that phone."

He handed it to her, and she thought about throwing it out the window but answered it instead. "Are you the bitch that got me into this mess?" she shouted.

There was a gasp over the line and a moment of silence. "Are you the bitch who stabbed me on the effin' four-oh-five?" Jessica responded.

"Hey, you got off easy. I could have twisted and slashed or stabbed you a dozen times like they do in the pen."

"Uh-huh," Jessica said over the line. "So do you have my low-life asshole boss with you, or did you steal his phone like you stole my money?"

"He's here with me. What would you like me to do with him?" Sadie said, sensing that the Asian bitch had no love for this man.

"Stab him the way you stabbed me, but do it a hundred times."

Sadie laughed. Did she have an ally? Her boss must be a major fuckhead if the woman she had stabbed wanted her to do worse to him. Clive looked over angrily, and Sadie pushed the knife into him a fraction of an inch, causing him to yelp.

"There's one of the hundred."

"Great. Let me talk to him. If he yells at me, give him another stab."

"Absolutely."

She handed the phone to Clive. Shaking, he put the phone to his ear.

"So you fired me, jackass," Jessica's voice came over the line loud enough for Sadie to hear.

"You were late," Clive said.

"I might've been there on time if I wasn't stabbed on the dammed freeway. But you never intended for me to make it to your house on time in the first place. You sent me on a fool's errand, knowing I would fail, so you could fire me because I wouldn't have sex with you. Isn't that true?"

"For God's sake, call the cops, Jessica. I'm being kid-napped! Ouch!"

Sadie drew blood on the second stab. One hundred times. Sadie thought about it. Powerful men and their abusive ways. Did they ever get the punishment they deserved, ever? No. And because of that they kept abusing, debasing, and destroying. Looking at Clive's clammy, ashen face, she saw her uncle with his large, rough hands, those boyfriends who had beaten and humiliated her, the dealers who whored her out in trade for their smack, the cops Tasing her after she was handcuffed, and today, that asshole judge taking her children away from her. She wanted revenge. She wanted to slice that dickhead's throat and watch him bleed out. But then he'd only die, and she'd be guilty of murder. No, that wouldn't do. He needed to live, but bear the scars of shame like she bore. What could she do to humiliate this bastard? A warm feeling rose inside of her. She should do it not only for herself, but for that angry Asian chick and all the other women in the future who he would undoubtedly try to screw over. A good turn, pay it forward, and all that hippie crap that helps the soul. But what? Then inspiration struck as she remembered a scene from a novel she had read in prison.

* * *

IN THE HOUSE, Jessica shook, feeling faint. She really needed a doctor. Like ten minutes ago.

"Let me talk to her," she said. She heard the phone rustle for a second.

"Hello," Sadie said.

"I have to call the paramedics before I bleed out. Do you have a plan?"

"None at all."

"Are you guys still heading to the Graumann's Chinese?"

There was a pause before Sadie said: "For the moment."

Jessica flattened out the crumpled paper she had found in the Oldsmobile.

"I have your paperwork, Sadie Bitterman. The judgment about your children." There was a moment of silence. Jessica decided to continue. "I can identify you, but—"

"But what? They'll find out who I am eventually."

"But I'll give you time to run. Maybe find your children. There's a Metro station at Hollywood and Highland. When the limo lines up for the red carpet, it will take half an hour at least. Jump out and run for it. You're on your own from there. But promise me one thing."

"What's that?"

"Promise me that somehow Clive Winterborne won't be able walk the red carpet tonight."

* * *

SADIE LOOKED AT Clive, pale and shaking. What kind of monster was he?

"I'm not one who usually questions a favor, but what did that son of a bitch do?" she asked over the phone.

"He's a total sleaze. Been hitting on me and throwing tantrums. Since I haven't had sex with him, he's firing me. Of course, if I had, he would have fired me anyway. He uses people and throws them away. He's awful."

Sadie felt a lump in her throat. That was her life. Getting screwed and used by slime like him. It started with Uncle Carl when she was five and then the unending line of predators who followed. "Consider it done."

She hung up the phone and reached toward the wet bar. Anger spread inside her like fire on gasoline. That reptilian part of her brain activated again.

"Now listen here—" Clive started to say, but was cut off when the champagne bottle Sadie had grabbed connected to his temple. He was out cold.

* * *

JESSICA CALLED 911 and then crawled into the bathroom where she hid her dismissal letter and Sadie's court papers, wedging them behind the toilet. There was no peroxide or first aid kit in the bathroom either. She crawled back to the office before a wave of blackness overtook her and she shut her eyes, floating into the dark.

* * *

WHEN CLIVE'S LIMO pulled up to the red carpet, only half of the photographers fixed their lenses on the door. It was only a producer, not a star. Those lucky ones got the shots of Clive Winterborne, unconscious and naked, hogtied with his own belt and propped up on his knees with the words "I ABUSE WOMEN" written in red lipstick across his chest. The driver, recovering from his shock, shut the door a couple of seconds later. Within minutes, pictures of Clive circulated throughout the internet.

* * *

JESSICA OPENED HER eyes slowly. Everything hurt. Florescent light stung her eyes. She turned to see needles in her arm and a police officer standing over her. He was tall, kind of cute. Then she noticed she was wearing a paper smock under blankets in a hospital bed. Oh God, she thought, I must look horrible.

"Ms. Tan?" the man asked.

"Yes," she croaked. Her throat was desert dry.

"Do you know the woman who stabbed you?"

Jessica blinked, and then shook her head. She needed to only remember the things that happened on the 405. "Never saw her before. Did you catch her?"

The officer shook his head. "But don't worry. We will." He pulled a small notebook from his pocket. "Can you tell me what happened yesterday?"

She gave him all the details until she stumbled into Sadie's car and started driving. He looked at her with an open expression like he wanted more. "I don't remember anything after that. At least so far."

The officer nodded thoughtfully and handed her his card. "If you remember anything else, give me a call."

She held his card. Officer Dan Trumble with his phone number and LAPD badge number. He nodded and left. Would he find out Clive had fired her? That she had consorted with the woman who had stabbed her?

The door opened, and Debbie from the production office walked in, her heels clacking on the tile.

"Oh my gawd, darling. How are you doing?"

"I hurt, all over."

"Oh honey, I'm so happy you're alive. Did the officer tell you about Clive?"

Jessica sat up. Her stomach screamed. "No, what happened?"

Debbie told her how Clive's notorious entrance had marred the premiere. "The driver said he ignored all the noises he heard because Clive has a reputation for doing weird things in the back of limos. He's always been a pervy creep, but now a bunch of women are talking to the media about how he screwed them over. Corporate canned his ass this morning, thank God."

"He's gone?"

"Nobody wants to touch him. You stay away from him. He's toxic."

Jessica nodded, her thoughts swimming slowly. She was probably pumped full of Demerol. He had it coming. He deserved this humiliation, right?

"Hey," Debbie said touching Jessica's shoulder. "Don't worry. We're keeping you, and you've been promoted to associate producer. There is always a silver lining, right?"

Jessica heard the word "Really?" escape her lips.

* * *

"MOMMY, WHEN ARE we getting ice cream?"

"After we pick up your brother, Tyler."

"Marcus?"

"No, your real brother, baby doll. Edgar. Not that fake family. Now just hush for a moment."

Sadie looked at her watch and then stared at the school doors waiting for them to open any minute. They sat in a Toyota Corolla, which she had jacked from a Ralph's in Studio City that morning. Then she had exchanged the license plates with another Corolla outside a beauty parlor in Van Nuys. She hoped it would buy her a day or two. The tricks you learn in prison.

She had picked up Tyler from kindergarten at noon, grabbing him at recess before the teachers could react.

Now she watched while several parents, mostly rich bitches, stood by their expensive cars, chatting at each other like idiots.

A bell from inside rang, and the front doors flew open a few seconds later with children rushing out like water from a faucet. Sadie strained to find her son among the sea of kids wearing the same blue knit shirts. Then she spotted Edgar walking with another boy. He had a backpack slung over his back on one shoulder. Sadie felt her heart tug. Her baby was becoming a man.

"Edgar!" she shouted.

He did a double take, looking at her and squinting. He then looked over to a woman standing by a Mercedes with a couple of other women. That lady had her eyes fixed on Sadie with her jaw hanging open.

"Come on, son," Sadie yelled. "Hurry."

Edgar took a hesitant step toward the foster mom and then turned, sprinting toward the Corolla. He hopped in the front seat, and Sadie gave him a bear hug before tearing down the road toward the 110. She hoped that her family would cross over into Mexico before the end of the day.

That was the dream Sadie chased. So vivid, so real, so perfect. She achieved it the only way she could, on Parker's couch. Her arm was still tied off. A needle lay beside her. The plunger already pushed through as chemicals coursed through her veins and her mind.

Quack and Dwight

I CONSIDERED NOT answering when I saw Shirley Chung's name on the caller ID. We'd been friends forever, going back to high school AP classes. She eventually went to law school while I got a PhD in psychology. Last time I took on a client for her, he was a six-foot-plus brute named Aaron. His junkie mother had dumped him with her abusive, drug-dealing brother when he was five. Shirley, the LA county prosecutor in Palmdale, was hoping that the fourteen-year-old would testify against his uncle, considering the multiple bruises he had on his backside from disciplining. The boy, however, had developed a paper-thin temper that craved any opportunity to explode. I discovered this when he lunged at me and broke my nose.

I answered the phone.

"I've got an emergency situation and need your help ASAP," Shirley said without a hello.

"When and what?" I asked, opening up my calendar.

"We're going to trial in two days, and we need help with a child witness."

My week was already full with my regular patients. Moving them would be an aggravating hassle.

"That's too soon, Shirley. You should've called me a month ago."

"We had somebody else, but he dropped out," Shirley said in an apologetic voice.

"Why?" That was crazy to take a contract with the county and then drop out unless there was a family emergency. You'd be blackballed for any sort of expert-witness testimony.

"Personal reasons, he says." Shirley's sarcastic tone let me know that she didn't believe him. "Regardless, we need you bad, and I've been authorized to double your hourly rate for an entire week, whether you're needed or not."

That was a lot of money, and I could always reschedule my patients.

"Tell me about this kid. Is he going to try to kill me?"

"He's eight. You can hold your own against that, right?"

"What's the situation?"

"We busted a meth cook and his wife several months ago. They had a trailer next door where they baked the drugs for a prison biker gang. We're coming down hard on the kingpin, a shitstain named Jack Taft. Neither the cook nor his wife will testify against Taft, but the boy says he saw him there several times and witnessed Taft giving his father money."

"Is he the only witness?"

"We're working on the mother. She gave testimony and then recanted. Somebody got to her. I've told her she'll never see her boy if she doesn't open up. If we can get her and the son's testimony, we can take the bastard down."

I was intrigued. "So Taft is bad news."

"The worst. He scares people shitless. We usually bust his crew, but never him. Nobody testifies against him. Ever."

"Is the boy in danger?"

"He shouldn't be. Gangs, as lawless as they are, usually don't kill kids. It's taboo. But . . ."

"But what?"

"It's the kingpin, so the rules are more . . . flexible."

A little voice inside of me screamed: *This isn't your problem, Ben. The money isn't worth it.* But another voice, the side of me that stood for law and order and craved to be a cape-wearing, crime-fighting crusader, said yes . . . out loud.

* * *

I CALLED MY part-time assistant, telling her to clear out my calendar for the week, while Shirley faxed over a contract with my rate doubled. The number looked nice. After I sent a signed copy back, she faxed over several dozen pages about the case. Shirley called before I could start reading.

"I need you to run up to Northridge and see Dwight. The address is in the packet that I'm sending you."

"Who's Dwight?"

"The witness."

Dwight. That was a name I had never run into in person.

"Get a sense of him and what he can do on the stand," Shirley continued. "Then bring him up to my office around noon. Got it?"

Shirley hung up before I could get another word in. She had the diplomacy of a bulldozer and attention span of a gnat. Driving up to the San Fernando Valley was never easy, but the Antelope Valley would be a serious hike. At least I'd be going against traffic coming from Santa Monica.

Reading the file, I couldn't help but shout, "Are you freakin' kidding me?" This had to be a practical joke, right? Had Shirley installed hidden cameras to catch my reaction? Dwight Adolf Lange. Nobody names a kid Adolf by accident. And the further I read, the more I confirmed my suspicions that the boy's parents were a part of a white-supremacist sect. At first I pondered God's twisted sense of humor, but then the more I thought about it, I felt like this was meant to happen. I was helping the universe by taking out the leader of this hatemongering organization. This was personal to me. My family lost several relatives to that paintbrush-mustachioed jackass and his nation of goose-stepping followers. Anybody evil or stupid enough to salute a Nazi flag will always be an enemy of mine.

Opening up my desk drawer, I searched through notepads, pens, and business cards until I found the small jewelry box in the back. I pulled out the solid-gold Star of David medallion and studied it. It still felt as heavy as the day I received it from my grandparents on the morning of my Bar Mitzvah. I clasped the chain around my neck. I wanted to see how little Adolf responded to that.

* * *

THE BOY'S SOCIAL worker, Nancy Gonzalez, met me outside of the group home in Northridge where the boy was staying. It was a typical two-story house set in a suburban neighborhood. Typical, except for the police officer posted outside the door.

"That isn't normal," I said, nodding at the officer scanning the street from a chair on the porch.

"No," she said brusquely. I had worked with Nancy before. She was sincere, somehow avoiding the cynicism that her work often breeds. A wave of resentment radiated off her. "Children aren't usually called on to testify against known murderers."

"The DA is trying to take that murderer off the streets."

"Do they really need a boy to do it?"

"None of the adults have stepped up."

"So the DA's going to use this kid for their own means and then throw him back to us with even more damage. Not much different from his screwed-up home life."

I didn't know what to say to temper her outrage. She couldn't change my mind since I knew I was doing a greater good.

"This prosecution has cost Dwight," Nancy said, glaring at me. "Two foster families sent him back after receiving threats. That's why he's at a group home with police protection."

"Surprised anybody wanted him, considering his middle name."

Nancy gave a half smirk. "Definitely makes a tougher sell. But Dwight is unique in spite of his biological parents." She touched my medallion. "Is this your way of starting a confrontation?"

"I want to see where the boy stands. If I'm going to work with him through this trial, he needs to know who I am."

Nancy shook her head. "You'll be surprised. Come on."

The officer nodded at me as we went inside the house. Apparently I didn't look like a threatening biker.

Nancy introduced me to the home's administrator, Jamal. Shaking the beefy yet kind man's hand, I couldn't hold back a smile. The boy's family would flip if they found out their son was being cared for by a black custodian. He led us to a small room with a couch, a few chairs, and a bookshelf. Posters with positive words and images of men and women exerting themselves by climbing mountains or running marathons hung on the walls. Nancy went over a few details with Jamal about me taking Dwight out of the home over the next few days. I gave him my best estimate about what our schedule might look like.

"But nothing's certain," I added.

"We're all on edge here with the cops hanging around our door, motorcycles rumbling past," Jamal said. "Sooner this is over, the better. Not just for Dwight, but all of us."

Nancy excused herself, dashing off to another case. Jamal stepped out for a minute and brought a scrawny boy into the room. He had a natural blond mullet ending with a rattail curl. His oversized Harley-Davidson T-shirt, faded to gray from years of use, hung loosely off his shoulders. No doubt a hand-me-down. His jean shorts looked filthy. A white-trash Aryan dream. Yet I couldn't detect an ounce of hate in those blue eyes.

"Dwight, this is Dr. Steinberg, and he's going take you up to Palmdale for that case."

"What happened to Sam?"

Jamal looked at me, and the boy followed his gaze.

"I'm taking Sam's place," I said, trying to convey confidence and authority. "He had to go out of town."

Disappointment crossed the boy's face as he looked down at his worn sneakers. Let down by an adult again.

"Hey Dwight, after this trial is over, how about you and me go out for some ice cream?" Jamal said, bending down to the boy's eye level. "What do you say?"

Dwight smiled, giving a nod. Jamal patted him on the back and left us alone.

"Take a seat, Dwight," I said, motioning to a sofa across from me. I wanted to know him better before we got on the road. See what I was going to deal with for the next few days.

I noticed his feet did not touch the ground. For an eight-year-old, he seemed small.

"Dwight, you can call me Ben." I reached over and shook the boy's reluctant hand. "So how are you doing?" I asked in a soft tone complemented with a smile and relaxed shoulders.

He shrugged, looking at his feet. I let a moment pass. Just before I was going to ask him about his upcoming testimony, he knit his brows in perplexed expression.

"How come you aren't wearing a white coat? Don't most doctors do that?"

"I'm not that kind of doctor."

"Do you have that metal thingy to listen to people's hearts?"

"No, I don't."

He paused for a second. "What do you do then if you're a doctor?"

"Normally I listen to what people say and then help them out in ways they need."

"So you're a duck doctor."

"A what?"

"A duck doctor," the boy said, twisting his face. "At least I think that's what Daddy calls them."

"Hmm." I made a mental note about the father's influence. The apple falling next to the tree. Wonderful.

Although it wasn't too pertinent to the case (the father had pled guilty to manufacturing meth and been sentenced to sixteen years for cooking over ten kilograms), I wanted to know more about the bastard's influence. "Tell me about your daddy. Do you miss him?"

The boy shrugged. "A little, I guess."

"You don't always miss him?"

The boy shook his head, looking at his scabbed knees. There was something on his mind. It looked painful.

"Why is that, Dwight? Can you tell me?"

Dwight shrugged, letting out a sigh. "I dunno. Sometimes he was mean. Especially to Mommy. But not always."

"Can you tell me what you mean when you say mean?"

Although the boy looked at a bookshelf full of Dr. Seuss and Shel Silverstein, his stare was a thousand miles deeper. "Sometimes, he'd yell at Mommy and throw things around the trailer. Especially if he'd been drinkin' or testing product with his friends."

Product was the word he'd heard for the crystal-methadone cooking in the nearby laboratory, according to the report. "Was that all he did, throw things?"

Dwight looked down at his hands, twisting them back and forth. "Slapped Mommy sometimes. And . . . hit her with his fists and then kicked her when she was on the floor. He usually cursed a lot too."

"Did he ever do anything to you?"

The boy froze, his little shoulders sunk inside of his oversized shirt.

"Dwight, look at me please." The boy turned his sapphire blue eyes my way. "Did your father ever hit you?"

"A little," he said meekly. His pale face whitened further. "But he spanked me more."

"How do you feel about that?"

The boy shrugged.

"Did your daddy say why he did it?"

He scrunched his face. "Sometimes it was because my

room was a mess or I left a toy or something outside. I tried to clean up, but he'd always find something wrong I did. Said he didn't wanna piss off JT."

I hated seeing children growing up with domestic violence, not knowing that life didn't have to be that way. Not knowing that it wasn't their fault.

"You know, Dwight, you should never be beaten by an adult. Even by your daddy."

The boy's face brightened. Shocked, I believed for a second that my words got through to him. That would be a first.

"Quack," the boy said.

"Excuse me."

"Quack. That's what Daddy says you guys are."

"Oh really?"

"Yeah, like a duck."

"Hmmm," I said, scratching my chin and giving him my best comical, perplexed look. "Do you think I'm a duck? I don't seem to have any wings." I looked at both of my arms.

The boy laughed. "No, of course you're not a duck. It's just a sayin'."

"Oh."

"But it would be cool if you really were."

"Really? Why's that?" I loved children's theories on the world.

Dwight's eyebrows knitted again. "I wouldn't mind being a duck 'cause I'd go swimming every day, and if there's any trouble, you know, I'd just flap my wings and fly away."

I leaned back, stunned with a lump in my throat. Damn this kid. He was breaking my heart with this sincere simplicity. I'd met hundreds of kids, but there was something special about Dwight. He had some unique quality that struck me hard. Expecting hateful confrontation, I encountered something totally different.

"You okay, Dr. Ben?" the boy asked.

"Sorry, just thinking. Continue what you were saying, Dwight."

"I wasn't saying anything. Just waiting for you."

I pushed my glasses up to the bridge of my nose and smiled. I needed to get back on track and do what the county was paying me to do. "Let's talk about a friend of your family, a guy named Jack Taft, okay?"

"JT," Dwight whispered, his eyes registering a hint of fear. Still, he bravely nodded.

* * *

WHEN JAMAL LED us to the front door an hour later, I noticed Dwight's face became rigid. He glared at the police officer from the open door.

"Wait just a second," the officer said, looking up the street through his mirrored sunglasses. He mumbled something into a microphone on his shoulder. In the distance, we heard the high-pitched whine of a motorcycle engine. The officer motioned us to step back inside with his left hand as his right hovered near his holstered pistol.

Dwight shook his head in disgust. Thirty seconds later, the officer, listening through his earpiece, told us it was safe to go to my car. I wondered if I should wear a bullet-proof vest for the next few days. After we were strapped in and on the road, I asked Dwight more questions. It was going to take us almost an hour to get the Palmdale DA's office.

"You didn't like that police officer, did you?"

"Pigs are stupid." He practically spat out the words.

I gripped the steering wheel, stunned at the hatred that he had not shown earlier. "Why do you say that?"

"That idiot can't tell the difference between a rice burner and a hog."

"How could you tell? We didn't even see any motorcycles drive by."

"Hogs engines rumble, rice burners whine," he said with a confident grin.

Had he heard that from somebody or come up with this insight on his own?

"So you know motorcycles really well?"

Dwight shrugged. "I know a little."

"What do you think about the police?"

Dwight shook his head and narrowed his eyes. "Hate 'em."

"Why's that?"

Dwight gave out an exasperated sigh. "'Cause . . . they're not nice."

For a kid who was abused by his father, neglected by his mother, and called "Little Shit" by Jack "JT" Taft, he was placing all of his anger on the one group who had freed him from a downward life trajectory.

"Is that because they arrested your daddy and mommy?"

He shrugged, signaling that was all I was going to get. I switched tactics, realizing he hadn't noticed my medallion.

"Anybody else you hate?"

Another shrug from Dwight as he stared out the window.

"What about Jamal? He's black."

"I don't care. He's a good person."

"Nancy? She's Latina."

He turned to me, his eyes furious. "What's your problem? Don't you know it doesn't matter about a person's skin color as long as they are decent?"

Dwight's directness surprised me. I felt like an asshole, being called out for trying to elicit racism from a child. "Where did you hear that from? I know it wasn't your daddy."

"Daddy hates a bunch of people. Mommy does too. But Grandma told me not to judge people until you meet them."

"Tell me about your grandmother."

Dwight stared at the cars we cruised by in the carpool lane. I had read a little about her in the file.

"I understand she passed away last year," I said in soft voice.

Dwight nodded, still looking away.

"I'm sorry."

He nodded.

"My grandmother died three years ago."

Dwight turned. "Sorry."

"Thank you," I said. "Know one of things I miss most? She used to make apple strudel for the holidays and pretty much anytime I'd come over."

"What's strudel?" Dwight asked.

"It's a pastry. Flakey and sweet with sugar, cinnamon, fruit and jam. I've eaten other strudels, but nobody made them better than my grandmother."

Dwight nodded, his eyes telling me he understood.

"Grandma made really good peanut butter cookies," he volunteered.

"You miss her?"

"Yes." His eyes glistened as he held back tears.

"Anything else you'd like to tell me about her? Sounds like she was a wonderful woman."

"Yeah, she was."

As Dwight talked about his grandmother, he filled in the blanks, helping me understand what made him tick. His father, Gerald, had only recently come back into Dwight's life. He'd started a six-year sentence months after Dwight was born. His delinquent mother, Tracy, had dropped Dwight at her mother's house for weeks at a time. From what I could gather, the grandmother was a warm and nurturing soul. It seemed like her kindness rubbed off on Dwight. Then two years ago, Gerald was released. He took Dwight and Tracy and stuck them in a trailer in the Palmdale desert.

As if that wasn't bad enough, Dwight's grandmother, his only known relative, was killed in a traffic accident. She died coming up from the San Fernando Valley to visit her grandson. I sensed that Dwight felt responsible. The burden was too much for an eight-year-old to carry. The poor kid couldn't catch a break.

* * *

SHIRLEY AND HER colleague, a young guy named Tom, sat across from Dwight at a conference room table. I sat behind them, watching. It was a risky strategy to put a child up on the stand, but after our brief conversations, I believed Dwight had the grit to pull through. He might hate cops, but he was honest. The prosecutors were going to test the boy. If it didn't go well, then I would have to tell a jury reasons why Dwight could not stand as witness while also pushing for his statement from nine months ago to be included. Dwight's identification of Taft from a six-pack of mug shots and his statement that the notorious kingpin had visited the meth lab several times had led to Taft's arrest.

Shirley started with questions about Taft being at the house and inside the lab. She provided photographs of the locations for Dwight to look at and confirm. He also reconfirmed he'd seen Taft paying his father and nick-named Dwight "Little Shit."

Tom followed with a vicious cross-examination.

"Are you certain it was Jack Taft, not another biker friend of your father's?"

"It was JT."

"Is there anybody else you know with the initials JT?"

Dwight thought about it. "No."

"What about Justin Timberlake?"

"Come on, Tom, objection," Shirley said, looking like she wanted to throw a pen at him.

"You know they're going to try to trip him up with those initials."

Shirley scribbled out a note. "You're right, I'll have to define JT better on my end."

They continued like this, Tom confounding Dwight with questions about his certainty of specific events.

Dwight looked at me from time to time, and I gave him a supportive "man" nod, letting him know he needed to stay strong.

After Tom was finished, Shirley started over with her questions, trying to preemptively neuter Tom's most potent inquiries. On his cross-examination, Tom came up with a new set of questions to boggle Dwight.

"How can you be sure you saw Mr. Taft give your father money in the middle of the night? Wasn't it dark outside?"

I stopped Shirley before she started a third round.

"We need to get Dwight some food. He didn't have lunch yet."

"The kid is a champ," Shirley whispered to me. "What did you do?"

"Nothing. We just talked." I glanced to make sure Dwight wasn't behind me. "We bonded over our grandmothers."

Shirley and Tom conferred over notes, while somebody in the office made a run for In-N-Out burgers and shakes. Dwight came over and sat next me.

"You're doing a great job, Dwight."

"Thanks."

He stared at a point below my mouth.

"What's that?" he asked, touching the Star of David around my neck. "I was going to ask you earlier, but I forgot."

I too forgot about the medallion hanging in front of my open collar. A feeling of panic hit me. I looked over at Shirley and Tom, fine tuning their notes. If I told him I was Jewish, would Dwight flip out on me? Would he feel betrayed and then scuttle his testimony. The prosecution's star witness tanking because of my heritage? I had planned to tell the Neo-Nazi spawn about my background, but I got distracted with his duck theory and all-around personality. Sure, Dwight believed you shouldn't judge somebody by their skin color, but he had blanket hate for cops.

Would he feel the same way about Jews? A community of people with different beliefs than his own.

"It's nothing . . . just something I wear," I said, stuffing the medallion under my collar. I felt an overwhelming sense of shame and cowardice.

He wanted to ask more questions, but probably sensed my discomfort. The food came in moments later, and we ate non-Kosher deliciousness.

* * *

WE DIDN'T LEAVE until after eight p.m., when Shirley declared they were "bulletproof." I hadn't paid too much attention as I had spent hours chastising myself instead of watching the testimony. I was determined to tell Dwight who I was when we got into the car.

As we were making my way out the door, Shirley mentioned that the mother, Tracy, might be willing to testify.

Dwight's exhausted demeanor flipped into excitement. "Does that mean I'm going to see her?"

"I'm not sure, Dwight. I'm going over to Chino tomorrow to see if she wants to help us out. I hope so," she said, mussing his hair.

Driving from Palmdale back to Northridge, we were mostly silent.

"Do you think my mom will testify?"

"I hope so," I said truthfully. It would take pressure off Dwight, and I could wipe my hands clean of this case. I remembered the promise I had made to myself. I had to do it, this case be damned.

"Got a question for you, Dwight."

"Okay."

"What do you think about Jews?" I tried to keep my voice nonchalant, but I'm sure it had some residual emotion in it.

"Why?"

I was sure the last thing Dwight wanted to do was to answer another series of questions.

"I'm curious."

"You're talking about those people who own all the banks and movies?"

I was breathless. Dwight's racist father had already indoctrinated him in spite of his grandmother's best countermeasures. I felt the urge to pull over and lecture him about stereotypes. But I needed to explore further. Was there hate? "What else do you know about them?"

Dwight leaned back, thinking. "Well, Daddy says they're the people who killed Jesus and control the world. That's why he hates them."

"Do you know any Jews?"

"I don't think so."

"Do you hate Jews?"

"I don't know." Dwight looked perplexed. "I'd need to meet one to make up my mind."

I couldn't help the huge laugh that escaped my lips.

"What's so funny?" Dwight asked, hurt.

"Nothing, I'm sorry," I said, wiping tears from my eyes. Though I lost it, I managed to keep the car on the road. "Got a trivia question for you. Did you know that Jesus was a Jew?"

Dwight blinked twice as his mouth opened. His mind was blown. "Are you fooling me, Dr. Ben?"

"Not at all. Mary was his mother, and you can trace her ancestry all the way to Moses."

"Wait, you're saying Moses was a Jew too?"

"He most certainly was."

Dwight rubbed the back of his head, flipping his rattail up and down. He was thinking hard.

"Can I tell you something else, Dwight?"

"If you want."

I lifted the medallion from my collar. "This is the Star of David." I pulled the chain over my head and handed it to him. He held it up in his hand, trying to look at it in the passing streetlights. I turned on the overhead light so he could see it better.

"Looks cool. Is it real gold?"

"It is. It's also a symbol of Jewish identity."

Dwight did a double take as his eyes almost bugged out of his head. Then he narrowed them, examining me. "Does that mean . . ."

"It means I'm a Jew."

"But . . . but you don't look like one."

"What does a Jew look like?"

Dwight took a few seconds, trying to recall the racist propaganda he'd encountered. "Aren't you supposed to have a big nose?"

I smirked. "It isn't small."

"What about a big hat and long beard and stuff like that?"

"That's a more strict, orthodox sect of Judaism. Most of us don't do that."

Dwight nodded, but it was obvious he didn't comprehend what I was saying. Regardless, he didn't hate me. He kept looking at the star, trying to comprehend it. I wondered why I cared about an eight-year-old's opinion of me.

* * *

PULLING INTO DWIGHT'S neighborhood, the road was blocked by police cruisers. Firemen, glowing in the red flashing lights of their fire trucks, sprayed water on the smoldering group home.

"What happened?" Dwight asked.

"I don't know." I pulled out my cell phone, remembering that I had turned it off inside the conference room since there was no reception. Pressing the "on" button, I waited for the software to boot up.

Somebody knocked on Dwight's window. We both screamed like we were in a haunted house. It was Nancy. I rolled down the window.

"What happened?"

"The home got firebombed. I've been trying to call you." She motioned with her eyes for me to get out of the car.

My phone finally engaged. There were seven messages on it. Dwight looked unnerved, twisting the star in his fingers.

"I'll be right back." Dwight's eyes widened. I pointed to his hands. "Hold on to that for good luck."

He hinted a smile. I got out of the car.

"How did it happen?" I asked in a whisper. "Where were the police?"

"They were here, but that gang sent a decoy, popping off shots and getting the officers to pursue him. Another a-hole came through seconds later and threw the firebomb."

"Is everybody okay?"

"They are. Jamal got the kids out in time."

I looked over at my BMW. Dwight clutched the star, his eyes locked on mine.

"What's going to happen to Dwight?"

"I've been working on it, but it's late and he's a high risk. Most families won't take him. He needs a witness protection program or—"

My phone rang. I answered. "Shirley, did you hear?"

"Yes. I've talked to Nancy."

Nancy raised her eyebrows at me as if saying there was one more thing.

"I need a huge, crazy favor from you," Shirley continued.

"What's that?" I asked, realizing our friendship had been a one-way street for a long time. But it was that way with most people. A constant pleaser. A man who will make others happy, even at the loss of my own personal identity. I'm not sure if it came from anticipating my mother's mood swings or from fitting in with the public school cool kids or combinations of that and more. I'd spent years of my life analyzing this fault, contenting myself with the argument that I could have much worse flaws like egomania or substance abuse. Shirley's firm yet cautious voice brought me back to the present.

"I need you to take Dwight home to your place. Just for tonight. I'll get a couple of officers posted there so it'll be safe."

"I can't put Rachel in danger."

"Nobody knows about you yet. Please, Ben, Dwight has bonded with you. Over grandmothers, remember?"

Although Shirley's manipulation was obvious, as I looked into Dwight's frightened, trusting eyes, I knew I had to say yes.

* * *

WHEN I CALLED my wife, Rachel, and told her about the situation, she was less than thrilled. Yet she didn't put up as much resistance as I had expected.

"One more thing, Rach. Can you check the freezer and see if we've got any strudel in there?"

"Why?"

"I'll tell you when you meet Dwight."

* * *

I SPOTTED AN unmarked police car when I pulled into our driveway. Stepping inside the house, my beautiful wife was waiting for us in the kitchen.

"Dwight, I want you to meet my wife, Rachel."

I saw strudel sitting on the table, but she didn't mention it. Her mouth was open, as she scanned the boy from his blond mullet to his stained T-shirt and scabby knees. Dwight wasn't the boy she had had in mind.

He held out his hand to her. "Nice to meet you, Dr. Rachel."

"Oh no, I'm not a doctor. Just a lawyer," she said, coming back to her senses.

Breathless for a moment, I feared Jewish-lawyer stereotypes escaping Dwight's mouth.

"But don't lawyers have something special about them?" he asked.

Rachel gave a wide-eye grin. "I have a Juris Doctor degree, but——"

"See, you're a doctor, just a funny-sounding one."

Rachel let out a snort. "I guess you could say so, Dwight. Come have some strudel," she said, pointing at the table.

"Like Dr. Ben's grandma used to make?"

"Well, it's not as good as hers," Rachel said with a little reluctance.

"Nobody's as good as Grandma Steinberg," I said, taking a dish and cutting a piece for Dwight. "But this isn't bad."

"Of course it's not," Rachel said, giving me her *watch it* look.

"This tastes awesome," Dwight said, after taking a bite.

In spite of the mullet, he had won Rachel over.

* * *

AFTER WE PUT Dwight to sleep in the guest bedroom with the smallest T-shirt I could find, Rachel and I talked in bed. I told her more details about the meth lab and the white supremacist background.

"I still don't understand how he turned out the way he did," Rachel said. "I didn't detect an ounce of hate."

"He had a loving and nurturing grandmother who raised him during a crucial development period."

"He knows we're Jewish, right?"

"Yeah. We're the first Jews he's aware of meeting. I think we're making a good impression for the tribe so far. We need to keep it up."

She pulled my face close and kissed me hard. Her eyes had a spark I hadn't seen in years. She locked our bedroom door and dropped her pajamas on the floor. Even though we had a guest in the room next door, we made quiet, vigorous love.

* * *

TWO DAYS LATER, I sat with Dwight outside the courtroom waiting for him to be called. Dwight wore a dark blue pinstripe suit that Rachel had bought from Macy's, along with a new wardrobe. She had taken the previous day off work and went on a shopping spree. She had also convinced him to get a haircut. A maternal side had emerged that I hadn't seen since we learned we couldn't have children.

Nervous, Dwight played with the star medallion, flipping it back and forth in his hands. My grandparents had given it to me at my Bar Mitzvah. I thought it was too gaudy at the time, but I cherished it now even if I didn't wear it often.

Towards the end of opening arguments, a sheriff's deputy escorted a scraggly woman in an orange prison jumpsuit across the lobby.

"Mom!" Dwight shouted. He leaped from the bench, running over to her. The escorting deputy tensed, but then relaxed. Dwight's mother, Tracy, bent down and opened her arms as far as her shackles would allow.

"Oh baby darling, I'm here. I'm here."

They hugged. She pulled back her long unkempt hair and wiped tears off of Dwight's face and her own.

"Look at you, honey darling. In a suit. You look so much like a man." She gave him another hug. Her emaciated arms trembled. "Listen here. After I do this . . . thing in there." Her eyes went over to the courtroom door. "They're supposed to cut me some slack. I'll get out in a few months, and after I jump through some hoops for them, I'll come and get you, all right? We'll be a family again."

Dwight nodded. Tracy embraced her son again, and I read fear across her face. Like she knew she made a promise she couldn't keep.

* * *

WE WAITED FOR an hour. Dwight was anxious, and so was I. He swung his feet back and forth while playing with the medallion.

"You doing okay?" I asked.

He nodded. "You think Mommy's going to be okay in there?"

"I think she can handle herself." I imagined she'd be an emotional wreck when the defense lined up all her prior drug possession charges and questioned her reliability. I patted him on the back. "Don't worry either. You're going to kick butt in there."

He nodded and handed the medallion back. "This is yours."

"Why don't you hold on to it for good luck?"

"Really?"

"You bet."

Dwight stuffed it into his pants pocket with reverence.

* * *

WHEN DWIGHT WAS called to the stand, he kicked butt, pointing out JT, even with his hair cut and beard shaved off. When the defense tried to impeach his testimony, Dwight didn't waver, saying unequivocally that he saw what he saw.

Shirley was delighted, giving me the thumbs-up more than once. At the end of Dwight's testimony, the defense asked the judge if they could meet in her chambers. They were looking for a plea bargain.

We celebrated with milkshakes and burgers at Crazy Otto's in Lancaster. Nancy called after we sat.

"I hate to do this to you, but can you hang on to Dwight for one more day? I'll have him in a home or a foster family by tomorrow, I swear."

"That depends on what Dwight says."

Dwight looked up from the food he was stuffing in his face, a question on his face.

"Would you want to stay another night with us, Dwight?"

Dwight grinned with a mouthful of fries and nodded.

* * *

WHEN I TOLD Rachel, she was delighted and proposed we

give him a home-cooked meal, considering he might not get one for a while.

"We ought to make it traditional too," she added. "He'll probably never get a Jewish meal again in his life."

Rachel gave me a shopping list, and, later that night, all three of us crowded into the kitchen. Rachel put together her family's famous raisin-and-carrot tsimmes while Dwight and I peeled and shredded potatoes for latkes. Rachel joked about "making a big tsimmes over Dwight," but it went over his head. We were also going to have brisket and matzo ball soup. I thought it was cheesy, but Rachel insisted on playing the *Fiddler on the Roof* sound-track.

"These recipes have been with our families for hundreds of years, Dwight."

"That's cool," he said, shredding the potatoes. "At home, we usually have microwave dinners. Sometimes."

I knew that sometimes meant he didn't get any food at all. The way he scarfed down burgers, it was like he might never get another meal in his life. While I fried the latkes, Dwight asked if he could help out.

"Do you want to set the table?"

"Sure."

Rachel handed him a stack of plates. He took them to the dining room, a place we rarely used. Usually we spent dinner zombied out in front of the TV. Hearing a crash, I turned to see Dwight wide-eyed with broken shards at his feet. His lower lip trembled as his body drew into itself.

I stepped away from the oven. "Dwight, it's . . ."

Dwight shot out of the room. I looked at Rachel. She was perplexed too.

"Dwight," I shouted, running after him. "It's okay."

He ran into the guest bathroom, locking himself inside.

"Dwight," I said in a kind voice, knocking on the door. "It's okay. We're not angry."

"I-I'm sorry," Dwight said through the closed door. "I didn't mean it. They slipped."

"They're just dishes," Rachel said. "I'll buy more tomorrow."

It took several more minutes to coax him out, with us swearing not to beat him over some lousy broken dishes. When he finally opened the door, the smoke detector wailed. All three of us jumped at the eardrum-piercing shriek. A latke was burning in the pan. Once the smoke cleared, we sat at the table and had a terrific meal.

* * *

"SO DWIGHT GOES back into foster care tomorrow?" Rachel asked in bed.

I nodded. "Nancy's supposed to pick him up before nine tomorrow."

Rachel took a deep breath and squeezed my hand. "I don't want him to go." Her eyes were big and imploring.

"I don't think we're ready for fostering yet."

"But if we don't step up, what will happen to him?"

"He'll go to a foster family or a group home."

"And if he breaks another plate with somebody else, what will happen to him? Will he get smacked around?"

"I don't know, Rachel," I said with a lump in my throat. "This is a big decision."

"Remember Bubbe Previn's story? How her Polish neighbors took her in as one of their own while the Nazis carted away the rest of her family . . . my family."

I gave a supportive nod, but her logic was apples versus oranges. "This isn't the Holocaust, though."

"No, but it's karma asking me to return the favor. That's why I was okay with Dwight staying the first night." She stroked my face. "Who knows, maybe this is the reason we couldn't have children in the first place."

My mind did backflips. We weren't atheists, but we didn't believe in an active hand of God either. Rachel's eyes had an intense determination rooted behind her unasked request. I've had my share of marital mistakes, but I am no fool.

We woke Dwight. Even though he was sleep-drunk, he came alive when Rachel asked if he would like us to be his foster parents.

"Yes, please," he said with enthusiastic nods.

We did a group hug. Tears streaked down Rachel's face while Dwight and I did our best to keep our manly emotions inside. We were starting a family.

* * *

THE FOLLOWING EIGHT months after taking Dwight as foster parents were the biggest upheaval in my life. I've had some of the most spectacular, life-fulfilling moments. Early on there were bumps as Dwight tested boundaries, subconsciously attempting to sabotage our relationship in order to test the elasticity of love. When we talked to him about stealing money or intentionally not coming home from school one day, he admitted to not knowing why he was acting out. He was just doing it. Slowly we built the bonds of trust.

Both of our parents, at first reluctant to accept a kid with a hateful lineage, were won over by Dwight, accepting him as a grandson. Rachel pushed us to become more active with the local synagogue. Rabbi Levy and the congregation took Dwight in as one of their own. We celebrated Hanukkah with a Christmas tree, and Dwight ended up with nine days of presents.

All the while, Dwight's mother, Tracy, was released, sobered up, joined NA, and took parenting classes. We never followed her progress because nobody thought she could make it through. Then a week before we were going to apply to have Dwight adopted, she moved to reclaim her son with the help of a lawyer. We were about to head out to a baseball game when Nancy called me with the news.

"After all we've been through, Nance, you can't let this happen," I said, keeping my voice down to a violent whisper as I walked into my office. Dwight and his new friend Alec were waiting for me in the living room, decked out in Dodger blue.

"I'm following the rules, Ben," she said flatly over the phone. She was too chickenshit to tell me in person. "I'm sorry."

"But who do the rules benefit? It's supposed to be the child, right? But there is no way that's going to happen if he goes back to her."

"Reunification between child and their biological parent is—"

"Nancy, stop. I know what the rules are and the motivations behind it, but tell me, truly, what are her chances of keeping Dwight?"

She sighed. That was not a good sign. "We're going to monitor her with weekly visits. And she has to pee in a cup every time. One violation and it's over for her. But she really has shown progress and a will to turn her life around—"

I hung up, not wanting to hear any more. I kicked a trash can and let out a primal shout. While Dwight was ambivalent about his father, I knew he missed his mother. But I remembered her strung-out look in prison orange. She was no suitable mother.

"What's going on?" Rachel asked, walking into the office. She still had on an apron from making a waffle brunch.

I shut the door. "We need to talk."

Rachel did not take it well. She said something I never thought I would hear her say in a million years.

"I'll kill that bitch if she takes Dwight away from me. I'll do it, Ben."

Her cheeks flushed, and her hands trembled. The savage look in her eyes said that she would rip the mother's heart out of her chest with her bare hands if she walked through the door. She had bonded to Dwight like a sealed envelope. To separate them would cause irreversible damage. Rachel read to him every night as he fell asleep.

The attentiveness that she gave Dwight, as he explained the minutiae of his day at school, was nothing like I had ever seen from her before. At times I vacillated between parental love and petty jealousy.

"She has a history of drug use and neglect, Rachel." I used my words very judiciously. "We should be able to win in family court, but it's not guaranteed. A sympathetic judge—"

"I'm going to call Sarah Levine," Rachel said, picking up her iPhone and scrolling through the directory. She was the attorney we were using for the adoption.

While Rachel talked to her, I came up with an idea. A horrible, awful idea, but it could save our family. Save Dwight from a life of destitution. A life of neglect.

When Rachel got off the phone, her eyes were moist. "Sarah's on it. But she says it could go either way." She bit her lip to hold back a torrent of tears.

"Rachel, I have a plan." Then I told her.

* * *

WALKING THROUGH THE steel door, Aaron saw me through the glass at the juvenile-detention center and stopped for a moment, squinting. Then an angry, surly mask morphed across his face as he recognized me. It was the same face he had when he attacked me more than a year earlier. That case for Shirley had netted me only a broken nose.

"What do you want, asshole?" he said after picking up the phone.

"Why do you say that, Aaron?" I couldn't help falling into therapist mode.

"'Cause of you I was put in isolation for three months. 'Cause of you, I ain't ever gonna see daylight until I'm eighteen."

"You attacked me, Aaron. There are consequences to your actions." He had already been on his way to juvie when I had been hired to see if I could pump some information out of him for the county.

"You were talkin' about my mama. That was none of your business to be askin' about her."

"I was just asking if . . ."

Aaron's eyes widened, anticipating an insult so he could go berserk. That wouldn't help me at all.

"Let me ask you something else. Do you like being in juvie?"

His eyes narrowed. He was ready to play ball. I was going to make a promise I couldn't keep.

* * *

I WAITED AT a Denny's in Palmdale. Sitting in a booth facing the parking lot, I had arrived thirty minutes early and watched the cars roll in. I was looking for a 1993 blue Pontiac Bonneville. That's what Shirley told me Tracy drove. That was the only thing I could get out of her about Dwight's mom, besides apologies. I got that information by saying that we wanted to make sure she wasn't driving by to kidnap Dwight.

"She testified, so we made good on our promise to cut her loose on probation," she had said. "Most of the time they get nailed for a violation within their first few weeks out."

That did not make me feel any better.

Ten minutes after our appointed time, the filthy junker pulled into the parking lot. I called Rachel.

"She's here."

"Where . . . Oh, I see her . . . Are you sure that's her?"

I squinted out the window. The woman that I had seen in the courthouse had been bone-thin with stringy blonde hair. If it weren't for the county-issued orange, I imagined she would have worn a Jack Daniel's T-Shirt with ripped-up jeans. This woman looked like her healthy, professional sister. She had her hair cut short and bobbed. She wore a cheap powder-blue dress with modest heels. She could have been a small-time real estate agent in a rural town.

Tracy walked inside, scanning the tables for me. I waved, and she looked at me as a cloud of confusion crossed her face. She hustled across the diner, dodging customers and waitresses. Her eyes looked from me and then to the empty booth seat.

"Is Dwight here?"

"He's not . . ."

She bit her lip and shook her head. I could tell she saw me as yet another obstacle in a string of disappointing life events. "You said Dwight would be here. That's why I came here. I want to see my baby boy. Where is he?"

The lie was the only way I could arrange a meeting with her. She looked like she was ready to leave.

"Take a seat, and let's talk about—"

"No, I'm jetting if he's not here. My attorney told me not to come here without him."

"He's with my wife," I lied. "I wanted to talk to you first and make sure everything is all right before you met with Dwight. If your attorney were here, it would be all legal mumbo jumbo. I have to say, I'm impressed. You seem to have made positive life changes. Please sit."

I waved my hand to the open chair. She hesitated, as an internal debate no doubt raged in her head. She had smiled briefly when I mentioned the positive change. I believe that is what got her to sit.

A young waitress came up with an air of unfiltered affability. "Hello, my name is Mindy. Would you like something to drink before I take your order?"

"Diet Coke, please," Tracy said in a low, apologetic voice.

"Can we get an order of mozzarella sticks, too?" I asked. The coffee I had been nursing was burning a hole in my stomach.

"Sure thing." Mindy scribbled the order and left.

"I don't have much money—"

"Don't worry, this is on me," I said. "Order whatever you'd like."

Tracy picked up the menu with hungry eyes, not much different from Dwight when I first took him out to eat. This would be a treat for her. She suddenly paused and closed the menu. "No, thank you. I've already eaten."

An obvious lie. I wanted to insist, but there was no need to offend her . . . yet.

I saw Rachel get out of our car and start to cross the parking lot. Tension racked my bones.

"So tell me about your progress." I also wanted to know how she could afford a lawyer too, but wasn't sure how to bring it up.

"Gradual. One step at a time. But I'm turning my life around now. And I mean it."

"Are you working anywhere?"

"At a beauty parlor, and I'm getting my GED. I used to have a beautician's license."

"That's great," I glanced out the window again, noticing Rachel approach Tracy's car with unnecessary caution.

Tracy's Diet Coke arrived. "The mozzarella sticks are on their way. Anything else I can get you?" the waitress asked.

"We're good for now," I said.

After the waitress left, Tracy leaned forward. "Tell me how Dwight's doing? He's been okay under your care?"

"Things have been great. We lov—care about Dwight a lot."

"Do you have pictures of him?"

"Sure . . ." I said, fumbling for my phone. I swiped through several pictures, skipping snapshots of him wearing a yarmulke at the synagogue or wrapped in a tallit with my parents at Passover. I settled on pictures at Disneyland.

"My boy," she said, taking the phone from me. A sob escaped her throat. "He's growing so fast." She scrolled through a few photos when the phone buzzed. I snatched it back, giving a curt sorry.

It was a text message from Rachel. I was hoping it read *Mission aborted*. But instead, one word glowed on the screen. *Done*. My breath caught. The machine we designed was operational.

"Mr. Steinberg . . ." I didn't want to correct her with my PhD title. Her eyes were glassy with tears. "It looks like you've done a wonderful job with Dwight. Thank you. But I want . . ." Her chin trembled for a second. "I need my boy back. He's the reason I'm sober. The reason I'm turning my screwed-up life around. I need him if I'm going to survive."

She wiped away tears. Mindy showed up with the mozzarella sticks.

"And here are . . ." She saw Tracy and went silent. She gave me a sympathetic nod and scurried away.

"How soon are you thinking of taking Dwight back? Do you have a place to live yet?"

"Soon, I hope. I'm in a halfway house now. I had to sell the trailer to get a lawyer, but me and a friend are looking for an apartment."

I saw in Tracy's eyes desperate hope backed by petrified fear. Part of me, an emotional side, wanted to help her. But the other half, the rational, educated side, knew self-delusion and self-destruction were frequent roommates. Nothing good would come from handing Dwight over to Tracy.

"You know that my wife and I were thinking of adopting Dwight before we heard—"

"Thank you again for taking such good care of him. Once I get Dwight settled with me, maybe you two can come visit him." She grabbed her purse, ready to leave.

"Wait, I want to ask you something that been bothering me about Dwight."

Tracy glanced at the door, ready to bolt. "What?" she asked in a tired voice.

"His middle name, Adolf. Why did you name him that?" I held back from calling it the mark of Cain.

She sighed, leaning back against the booth. Her cheeks flushed while she stared at her hands. I noticed that she wasn't wearing a wedding band. "I was about ready to deliver when Gerald, Dwight's father, got arrested on his second robbery offense. He told me to name the boy Adolf because he knew he was going up to San Quentin and he wanted to get in with Aryans up there for protection." She shook her head. "Selfish bastard from day one."

"But why did you do it? He was in jail anyway."

"He told me I'd better 'cause somebody'd come and check." She looked at me with tears streaking down her cheeks. "Sure enough, a big biker came out to see the birth certificate about two months after Dwight was born."

She clutched her arms and shivered. Although she didn't say anything else, I could tell the biker got more than a look at the birth certificate. I didn't know what to say. I was speechless trying to comprehend what she had told me.

"Good night, Mr. Steinberg, and thank you again for looking after my boy."

I nodded. "Good night."

She rose and walked to the door. I called Rachel.

"Has she left yet?" my wife answered.

"We need to call this off."

"There she is."

"Rachel, wait."

She hung up on me. I threw a twenty next to the untouched sticks and rushed for the door. I saw Tracy's clunker make a right turn out onto the street. I ran to our BMW at the end of the parking lot. Rachel sat in the passenger seat, the blue glow of a cell phone silhouetting her face. When I jerked the door open, I heard her say, "Please hurry." She collapsed the disposable cell phone and glared at me with intense eyes, daring me to defy her.

"Everything is in motion."

I sank into the driver's seat feeling like I had inhabited somebody else's body. A dark, sinister man. A conspirator.

A life-wrecker. I couldn't believe what we had just done.

* * *

WE DROVE DOWN the road in silence. Rachel had her chin jutting out in self-righteousness. I gripped the steering wheel, keeping my eyes focused on the road.

"Over there." She pointed to the blue and red flashing lights more than two blocks away. "I think that's her."

I slowed down to fifteen miles an hour. Tracy's car was pulled over, and she sat on the sidewalk shouting something to an officer who shined a bright ghostly light in her face. A K-9 police cruiser was also there, and an officer led an eager German shepherd into the back of the Pontiac. Rachel squeezed my arm.

"It's happening," she said in a voice mixed with fear and hope, looking through the side-view mirror.

I did a U-turn two blocks away. Coming back we saw Tracy, cuffed and screaming a fury of words at two officers as they pushed her into the back of a squad car. The K-9 officer held a bag in his gloved hand as the other gripped the dog's leash.

* * *

WE WERE ON the highway heading home when Rachel let out a sigh, slinking into her seat. I tried to smile. As we got closer to civilization—Santa Monica, a place far away from meth dealers, filthy air, and tumbleweeds—an ill feeling crept upon me. *We did the right thing*, I told myself. We rescued Dwight from a fate of poverty and crime. A woman who had messed up her life. A woman who, even with the best intentions to turn her life around, would not pull it off. And what would happen? Dwight would suffered irreparable damages. Dwight, he was our boy now. I swallowed dryly and repeated to myself, *We did the right thing, we did the right thing*.

In the trunk lay the pile of Goodwill clothes I'd bought to try to blend in with the Palmdale culture, although it had not worked at all. Aaron's Uncle Lewis laughed at me.

"Hell, I would've thought this was a drug bust, but the cops wouldn't send no candy-ass like you in here. It's too obvious."

He made me pay out the nose for it. Three hundred dollars for a little plastic baggie of clear crystal rocks. Three hundred to ruin one life. Three hundred to give a better life to another.

"Hey, Ben," Rachel said, touching my arm.

I glanced over at my wife. By the concerned line on her forehead, she had something heavy on her mind. Was she finally feeling guilt too?

"Yeah?"

"I was thinking, once we get Dwight fully adopted, maybe we can look at fostering a little girl. What do you say?"

Final Testimony

HATCHER FLASHED HIS badge when the metal detector squealed. A sheriff's deputy exchanged his Glock for a ticket. He didn't notice the backup strapped to his ankle.

Minutes later, Hatcher took a seat on the witness stand, trading glares with the defendant, Bradley Turner. He had risked everything to bring this miscreant to justice. Today was his second day on the stand and probably his final testimony as an official cop. According to his lieutenant, Internal Affairs planned to take his badge and gun after the trial.

The judge called the court back into session, reminding Hatcher he was still under oath. Martin Dies, Turner's bloated attorney, stood. He wore a Rolex that equaled two years of Hatcher's salary.

"Detective Hatcher, we heard yesterday from the prosecution about how you harassed and hunted my client, accusing him of murders he didn't commit."

"Objection!" DA Cathy Martinez stood, stress lines carved across her face. Hatcher knew she and her assistant, Gary Something-or-other, had little faith that he could withstand cross-examination. He'd show them.

"Turner's a murderer," Hatcher said before Martinez could continue. "No question."

"Overruled," the judge said.

"Do you have evidence to support your claim?" Dies asked.

"I found plenty in his house. Knives, restraints, bloody clothes from several victims. It was a glimpse into hell."

He stole a glance at the jury. They were enthralled at

the details.

"Did you have a search warrant when you entered Mr. Turner's property?"

"Didn't have time. There could've been a girl inside."

"Didn't have time? Aren't there procedures to ensure that malfeasance on the part of the law doesn't occur?"

"I had probable cause. Lives were at stake."

"Was anybody else with you when you trespassed onto the property?"

"I didn't trespass, and I entered alone." He wanted to add, *That's what makes me effective.*

"No witnesses saw you enter?"

"Correct."

"So you could've planted evidence without anybody watching?"

Blood flushed Hatcher's cheeks. Dies was trying to make him into Mark Fuhrman. "I did not. I found what I found. Secured the scene and called it in."

"Says you. What qualifies you to break into a citizen's home without their consent?"

"He's a murd—"

"Mr. Hatcher, I asked what qualifies you to break—"

"I've been an officer of the law for twenty-three years. I've received several commendations—"

"We heard all that yesterday." Dies gave a dismissive wave. "Isn't it true that you are currently under investigation by Internal Affairs for stealing drugs from the evidence room and using them for your own consumption?"

Martinez objected, and the two lawyers argued before the judge overruled.

"Answer the question," the judge instructed.

Hatcher heard the whispering swish of water from the plumbing in the overheard ceiling, a cough in the hallway. Everybody watched Hatcher. He felt their stares boring into him, trying to examine a soul they could never understand.

There was no right answer, except to perjure himself,

which would only make things worse. Narcotics gave him the edge. Drove him harder than anybody else on the force to find the sociopath. Three sleepless months. It had wrecked everything in his life—an estranged wife with a restraining order and a daughter who denied his existence—but he caught Turner. The handsome trust fund alpha could have any woman, yet he preferred to abduct, torture, and kill runaways. American Psycho without a job. Idle time and money. Turner beamed a malignant, triumphant grin.

Hatcher cleared his throat. "I'm not allowed to discuss the current investigation."

"Really?" Dies acted confused. "If you stole drugs from police, how can we trust you?"

"Objection. Assumes facts not in evidence, badgering the witness . . ."

Martinez went on, but Hatcher tuned her out. He glanced at the jury box. A few worried, confused faces. Others seemed amused. But a couple of hard, angry glares met his eyes. He knew that look, total mistrust of cops. Now they had ammunition to hang a jury or, worse, declare innocence.

His body trembled. This was the end of everything. He had fucked up too big this time. He'd be imprisoned by year's end, while this sadistic murderer walked the streets inflicting more harm. All because of money-grubbing whore lawyers like Dies.

This couldn't happen. He slipped his hand into his pocket, palming a pill. Feigning a yawn, he dry-swallowed the speed. His heart slammed against his chest seconds later. His smile matched Turner's. He had the chemical courage to see this through.

"Detective Hatcher," Dies resumed after the objection was sustained. "Can you tell the jury if you've flunked a drug test in the past year?"

He held a piece of paper in his hand. Hatcher knew what it was. The test that revealed a cocktail of speed and coke in his system. How did Dies get it? Evil money greased a wheel somewhere.

At the prosecution table, defeat clouded Gary's face. He whispered into Martinez's ear. She nodded gravely. Were they thinking of offering a plea bargain? No way. He had sacrificed too much for that.

"Detective Hatcher, would you like me to repeat the question?"

Hatcher studied Dies's piggish face. "How do you live with yourself, representing murderous filth?"

"Your Honor." Dies looked like a man dealing with a child's tantrum.

The judge banged the gavel. "I'll remind the witness to only answer—"

Hatcher drew from his ankle holster and blew a hole in Dies's head. He placed a bead on Turner and for a quick second savored the wide eyes and open mouth on the rich kid's face before two in the chest knocked the bastard to the floor. Pandemonium filled the courtroom as jurors, lawyers, and the audience scrambled to the doors. A *whoop-whoop* filled the room as the judge tripped an alarm. Hatcher swiveled to the deputy sheriff, who had pulled his weapon.

"No need to kill anybody if you haven't before." Hatcher smiled at the young, trembling deputy. "I've got it from here." He raised the pistol to his own temple and glanced at Turner, dying alone in a pool of blood. "Justice served."

Not Sure Which Way I'm Headin'

WHEN BLAKE STEPS up to the microphone, the drunken audience of forty, give or take, chants a nickname he'd rather not have, "Haw-lee-wood, Haw-lee-wood."

He grins and waves to people he's known his entire life. There has been some good competition for once on karaoke night. That is, if you discount Allen Majors's unending, chalkboard-scratching version of "Stairway to Heaven" that nearly cleared out the joint. And how many times can you hear Toby Keith's "I Love This Bar" in a single night? Apparently there isn't a number since it was sung every other turn, each interpretation getting progressively worse as the beer continued to flow. Now it was time to put them all to shame and pick up some tail for the end of the night.

"This one goes out to the class of nineteen-eighty-eight."

Three or so alumni shout with pride. Would've been a time when those shouts would've shook the bar, but they've been dropping like flies over the years. Perhaps the hassle of finding Friday night babysitters, or maybe, though he didn't want to believe it, some of his friends who passed forty on their odometers decided to call it quits and ease into middle age, focusing only on retirement. Well, screw 'em. Blake's going to prove he still has all the swagger and intensity that he had when he was eighteen. Growing old is for pussies.

The karaoke machine's monitor flashes the name of the song, and the audience goes wild. Soft synthesizer chords—the dramatic album version of the song, not the

---

128

radio straight-up rock ditty—play on the speakers. Blake dons his serious face, holding the microphone with both hands. Drunken patrons clamber out of their chairs, crowding around the one-foot tall stage. Just like it used to be, almost.

"Not sure which way I'm headin'," he croons in his over-the-top Daniel Cloverfield impression. "But I've been around for sure." He drops out of character, pointing at Katie Pilgrim, Angie Smith, and Dawn Campbell. "I've been with you and you and you."

The audience laughs.

"You wish!" Dawn shouts.

He has, but she's with Glenn Walters tonight. Katie and Angie, however, smile back with big, longing, let's-get-out-of-here-and-do-the-nasty eyes. That's awesome. There will be competition tonight, which means either one is more likely to put out more than they do on their regular late-night booty calls.

As he sings about lies in old tunes, he searches the audience for any other single ladies. There's Janelle, but Clint McGeorge has his meaty paws around her. Cynthia and Kim are mashing their overripe behinds against gangly men with beat-up Sooner ball hats.

"But I've decided right now, I'm not waitin' any longer," Blake sings in a snarl, managing to keep it under a scream. Then he takes it down a notch. "I'm doin' it again."

The crowd shouts as a keyboard solos for a couple of bars. Blake holds back a smile, nodding in appreciation while keeping Cloverfield's over-the-top seriousness intact. He knows the Pale Serpent frontman's moves better than anybody else. At seventeen he recorded the MTV video on a VHS tape and watched it until the images were useless. This song was his anthem. This song made him believe he was too big for his hometown. Too big for Oklahoma.

He picks up the next verse about searching and not being satisfied. Yeah, it'll be either Katie or Angie tonight.

Both have let themselves go over the years, but who hasn't that's over thirty? He's been losing the battle with his beer belly recently. So which one? Katie gives better blowjobs, but Angie, if drunk enough, might let him stick it up her butt.

Blake growls the next line into the mic. He can feel the energy building in the room. The power of '80s hard rock is infecting everybody's soul. It's the message of free will and the pursuit of good times.

"Yeah I know how it feeeels." The hairs on his arms rise. Yes, he's going to do it. He's going to blow the roof off the Dusty Lanes bowling alley bar. Going to let all of Coal County know that he is Blake Henderson, and he is here to rock. "To stumble down the broken road of ideals."

Inhaling, he scans the audience, their eager faces ready for him to belt out the chorus. Then he spots a white-haired Asian man sitting alone in a booth. His face is hard. He is oblivious to the music, staring at Blake. Their eyes lock.

"I'm doin' it again by myself!" the drunken crowd shouts in unison. "I ain't gonna be put on nobody's shelf."

Blake stands silent, the microphone slipping from his fingers. It clangs to the floor. The man is older, but it's definitely him. For decades Blake has been trying to forget, trying to cleanse that horrific memory from his mind with booze and distraction. But the nightmares about that day still haunt him.

"Come on, Blake," Katie yells. "Sing it."

"Are you all right?" Angie asks, rushing up to him.

He blinks and looks down at her.

"Of course he is," Katie says, stepping up on the stage. "Here, let's sing this together, Blake."

He looks back to the booth, but the man is gone.

Katie screeches, "To stumble down the broken road of ideals." It is awful.

"You don't look well," Angie says, pulling Blake off the stage.

Katie grabs Blake's shoulder. "Wait, aren't we doing this together?"

Blake shakes his head, trying to get his senses back. People aren't singing anymore, but staring at him like his head's bleeding.

"I need a break," he tells Katie. Embarrassment reddens her face, but he doesn't care.

"Dude, you okay?" Clint asks. "You look as white as a ghost, man."

A crowd forms around him. Katie stops her screeching, and Robbie, the twenty-one-year-old DJ whose mother Blake grew up with, kills the music. Different folks tell him to sit and drink some water or ask him how many beers he'd had.

"Did anybody see that older guy sitting in the back?"

"That Chinese fella?" Clint says.

"He's Korean."

"How can you tell?" Angie asks.

"It's . . ." Blake starts, bringing his hands to his face to explain different features, but then he stops. How can he describe the differences? It's just something he knows. Besides, he would have never known Koreans or any other Asians had he not lived in California for a spell.

"Hell, they all look the same to me," Clint says.

"Don't say that," Blake says, harsher than he means to. "It's like saying people from Oklahoma and Texas are the same."

Clint's bearded face screws up tight, like he swallowed buttermilk thinking it was two percent. "Bullshit to that."

Blake feels his senses coming back. "Any of y'all see where that guy went?"

"We're all watchin' you," Angie says, grabbing his arm and shooting him those let's-do-it-in-the-bathroom-right-now eyes.

"Do you know that guy?" Katie asks.

Angie tightens her grip on Blake's arm.

"Not really," Blake says.

He unlatches Angie's hand and excuses himself. He needs to get out of the bar and see if Mr. Song is waiting outside. This has been a long time coming. Tonight might be his final breath of Oklahoma air.

Gravel crunches under Blake's Ropers as he steps into the crisp, autumn breeze. He recognizes all the cars and trucks. Nothing looks unfamiliar. Except for Robbie's Honda and Katie's Mazda, every other vehicle is American made. He leans against his Silverado and stares up at the sky. Even with the parking lot light, he can still see thousands of stars. Something he couldn't do in LA. Every once in a while, on a clear night after it rained, he was able to see the North Star or maybe Venus. He shakes his head. Why didn't he just plant roots like everybody else instead of being that idiot rambler who takes care of himself?

He hears Allen Major start into "American Pie." That'll clear out the bar in a hurry, causing the patrons to either call it a night or take a smoke break even if they don't light up. He reaches for his keys as the bar door opens. If he doesn't skedaddle immediately, there'll be questions he doesn't want to answer. Like what really happened in LA, the true story he omits when talking about his adventures in the early '90s. That history is supposed to stay over there and never make its way east. People here wouldn't understand.

He's backing up when Angie flags him down. Good Lord, she's persistent when she's horny. He rolls down his window.

"Not coming back in?"

"Don't got it in me. Headin' home."

"You're not looking too good. Anything I can help you with?" Her eyes say anything and everything is on the menu.

"Ain't in the mood tonight, Angie. Sorry."

"I don't mean that. I mean, we don't have to have sex. I can tell there's somethin' botherin' you, and you've been there for me a time or two. Seems like I could help you out some."

Blake can't think how he's ever helped her at all. He caused the divorce between her and her high school sweetheart, Jack. But then again, they'd been hating each other for several years, even if they didn't admit it. Maybe he did them both a favor with that affair.

He doesn't know where Mr. Song went. Since he isn't at the bar, maybe he's waiting at the house for Blake, or maybe he called the sheriff's department and they're coming to arrest him. He could run, but he's tired of that. Maybe he should enjoy his last moments of freedom.

"Sure," Blake finally says. "Let's head over to McCoy's in Tupelo." He unlocks the passenger door. "Oughtta be quieter there."

* * *

BLAKE DRINKS HIMSELF stupid, ordering whiskey shots with beer chasers, one after another. Angie asks him about the "Chinese, I mean, Korean guy," but he doesn't budge.

"Don't know what you're talkin' about," Blake slurs.

"What about that scar on the top of your ear, did he do that?"

Blake instinctively touches his left ear but then shakes his head, keeping his eyes away from Angie. "Refill," he shouts at the bartender.

By the time the bar closes, Blake's too drunk to screw, but that doesn't stop Angie from trying in his truck's cab. She's stubborn to the core.

"You should look into some Viagra," she says, zipping up his Wranglers. "It happens to all men, you know."

Blake shouldn't be driving, but he does, ignoring Angie's pleas to let her take him home. He drops her off at the bowling alley and promises to call when he gets home. Playing a mixed CD of '80s metal tunes with the windows rolled down, the air blasting a frigid forty-degrees, he manages to navigate home.

Blake takes out the .38 revolver he keeps locked in the

glove box and wobbles out of his truck. He studies his neighborhood street for a few moments. From what he can tell, there aren't any different cars parked outside.

He unlocks the front door of his pre-war two-bedroom home. It only cost thirty-six thou. Californians would have forked over mid-six figures for some rickety clapboard structure like this. Ree-dic-u-lous. He takes a deep breath and opens the door with his Colt pointed ahead of him. He turns on the light, scans the living room, swinging his pistol left and then right.

Good Lord, he's wasted. Too slow to win any gunfight, that's for sure. He locks the door and searches the rest of house. It's empty as far as he can tell, and nothing is out of place. Not the empty Bud bottles and microwave containers with remnants of food on the coffee table, not the clothes dropped in piles all over the floor, not the copies of *Hustler* in the bathroom, not the stack of unpaid bills scattered across the kitchen table. And not the only respectable thing in the whole place, the picture of his ten-year-old daughter, Meghan, which hangs on the hallway wall. Yet he feels a presence. As if somebody has been there.

He sleeps that night with the Colt beside him. In his mind, the repressed memory, the reality of what happened, comes back more vivid than ever. It starts with the long drive across the I-40 with barely enough money to buy gas and burgers. Then the struggle to make ends meet, working odd jobs, often paid in cash for helping out on sets for low-budget films and videos. Finally he starts working toward his goal of forming a heavy metal band . . .

* * *

STARTING UP A band in Los Angeles during the late '80s wasn't a tough thing to do. Guitarists, bassists, drummers, and even keyboardists littered the Sunset Strip. Throw a beer bottle in the Rainbow Room, and it would bounce off a couple musicians before landing in a groupie's lap. But anytime Blake found anybody good, they'd get snatched up by a bigger band a couple days later.

His band, Avenging Justice, played several gigs in East Hollywood dives. Obscure bars claiming Mötley Crüe and Guns N' Roses got started there, with stages so tiny that Blake couldn't move without knocking into his bandmates. It was miserable, but eventually they got some traction. A few record label reps talked to them, and, in late 1991, they were gearing up to make an EP.

Blake's future, at that one moment in time, was neon-red awesome. A big-time manager who promised to sign them held a massive blowout at his mansion overlooking Sunset Boulevard. His place was stocked with booze, well-endowed women, and cocaine. Admiring the floor-to-ceiling windows and red leather furniture, clarity walloped Blake across the face. Success looked like this. He couldn't wait to nail the demo and collect the rewards.

The demo never happened. Something else did.

A bunch of scuzzy kids in Seattle started making waves. "Smells Like Teen Spirit"—what a bunch of muttering, nonsensical horseshit—took over the airwaves, and everybody, against all logic, loved the crap. Heavy metal, or hairbands, as they were being called with derision, was the old shit.

Everything about Blake—from his tan skin and long platinum hair to his anthems designed to rock arenas—became passé. People didn't want to feel good anymore. They wanted to be depressed and suicidal. Thank you very much, Mr. Cobain.

A year later, Blake lived in a termite-infested house in East Hollywood with two guys from other disbanded metal bands. Greg was a fair-skinned redhead from Louisiana and had been the lead singer in a band called Slickk. Sam was a thick bassist from Tennessee who could only play a few chords and loathed country music. All three of them hated their lives. Dreams that were close enough to grasp had been snatched away.

Many of their musician friends tried to remake themselves as "alternative" rockers (but not rock stars, heaven forbid) or packed up and followed their father's footsteps, laying bricks, building cars, whatever. Yet the three of them still believed in the heavy metal music of their youth. Unfortunately, nobody else did. With no gigs, they were broke, and work was impossible to find. Blake's blow-dried hair garnered more giggles than the respect he used to get walking down Sunset.

Blake hated the music industry for turning on a dime. He hated the fickle fans for turning their backs on the greatest genre in rock music. And mostly, he hated Los Angeles. The evil city used people, sucking them dry until they were nothing but skin and bones, and then tossed them to the curb. He hated his roommates too, because it took nothing to set them off. A rage festered, increasing in toxicity every day. In retrospect, he had all the brooding resentment to front a grunge band. But that didn't happen. The Rodney King Riots did.

It was late in the afternoon when the verdict came from the Simi Valley courthouse. Greg and Sam lounged on the broken-down sofa watching the TV coverage. Blake slathered generic peanut butter across stale bread for a late lunch. Sam let out a whoop of joy. He couldn't have been any happier than if the Tennessee Volunteers had won a national championship. The cops who had beaten Rodney King senseless were acquitted.

"Toldja. We never saw the beginnin' of that tape. I know Rodney went apeshit on them cops before that dude started tapin'. The jury proved it's true. And I know from experience them darkies are crazy violent. I mean you can't look at some of 'em without gettin' smacked down in Memphis. I kid you not."

Blake felt outrage bubbling inside his chest. "Dude, this isn't about race."

"Hell, it's not," Sam said.

"No. It's another blatant example of one person gettin'

screwed by the soul crushin', almighty power of Los Angeles. Cops can beat the crap out of you on camera with millions of people watchin' and it doesn't matter, because Los Angeles always wins. It's just too fuckin' big."

"I have no idea what you're talkin' about," Sam said.

Greg shook his head. "I don't know what's gonna happen next. But it can't be good."

"Y'all are idiots," Sam said. "We won today, if you want my opinion."

"No, we don't want it," Blake said.

"Never have," Greg added. "But it's never stopped you from givin' it to us."

"Screw you guys," Sam said, turning back to the TV.

The newscast was already interviewing outraged African-Americans. Blake felt the same way as they did. The ruling was an injustice, a total travesty. He rushed out of the house to get some air.

East Hollywood felt eerily quiet. The neighbors would usually be up and about by this time in the afternoon: Russian immigrants, impoverished transvestites, failed actresses turned hookers, retirees of a bygone Hollywood era, and washouts like himself on the verge of losing everything. But today he felt like the only person outside. Even the birds kept quiet.

He walked, one foot following the other. The few people who Blake saw glanced at him with suspicion. He wanted to shout "fuck you" and chase those assholes down the block.

The silence that had stilled the air was replaced by sirens and helicopter rotors. Not just a single ghetto bird, but a flock of them. When he made it to Western Avenue, he turned south, walking past the windows of furniture stores displaying modern couches and chairs. He would love to replace his broken, filthy furniture with any of those pieces. Then he spotted a red leather couch, exactly like the one at the manager's party. It sat behind a floor-length window, displaying all of its elegant beauty. It wasn't logical, but Blake knew that if he owned that couch, things would be different. That couch was the signature of success.

A line of police cars, followed by fire trucks and an ambulance, flew past, weaving through traffic. Blake continued down the street. He stopped at a strip mall, where a group of customers and Korean merchants of massages, liquor, and kimchi watched the gaggle of helicopters hovering in the distance. It was easy to tell who were the customers and who were the sellers by the hungry, opportunistic eyes versus the fearful, enlarged pupils.

When Blake returned home, he was surprised to find the front door locked. Greg opened the door, a Ruger pistol in his hand.

"You should see the shit goin' down," he said. "It's nuts, man."

"Toldja!" Sam said, pointing at the TV where a live helicopter feed showed swarms of people rioting on the streets. "Them blacks are crazy."

Blake and Greg joined Sam on the couch, watching in slack-jawed silence. It was chaos. Anarchy on live TV. Cars overturned and set ablaze. Store windows smashed and businesses looted.

Blake felt outraged out of common decency, but there was also a lining of satisfaction. LA had this coming.

* * *

THE NEXT MORNING, whatever calm had been promised by the city leaders was over. A resurgence of anger and opportunism played out live in front of a TV-viewing audience. The looting had spread.

"That's our store," Greg said, pointing at a Thrifty with swarms of people running in and others coming out carrying whatever they could manage—diapers in one arm, a case of beer in the other.

Outrage swelled inside of Blake. He paid for his beer,

and it wasn't cheap. He turned to Greg.

"You wanna go shoppin'?"

"Thinkin' the same thing."

Blake grabbed his puny .22 pistol and stood. He knocked on the bathroom door where Sam was stinking up the house.

"We're grabbin' some supplies. Be back in a few."

"Wait a sec," Sam shouted as the toilet flushed. The door swung open, and Blake had to step back. "Where y'all goin'?"

"Thrifty. There's a free-for-all happenin'," Blake said. "I don't want to be the last one there, gettin' a bag of broken potato chips."

"I'm comin'."

"I don't think——"

"Fuck you, man. I'm goin' with you guys."

* * *

BLAKE PULLED HIS TRUCK into the parking lot five minutes later. He had heard the word *pandemonium* before and never thought he'd ever use it, but that's what it was. Complete pandemonium. If anything, the crowds had tripled since they'd seen the coverage. As if the news had advertised, *Come and get it, folks!*

Blake glanced at Greg, who gave him the same hesitant look.

"Let's do this thing. Woo!" Sam shouted. He jumped out of the truck, turning to Blake and Greg. "Come on, pussies. Let's get some shit."

"So much for law-and-order Sam," Greg said.

They followed the whooping and hollering Sam. It was dark inside, but Blake knew where to go. He grabbed a paper sack from the checkout counter and headed to the liquor section. He could find it in complete darkness. He grabbed bottles of what should have been Jack Daniel's and Jim Beam. He also hoped he was stealing some Smirnoff. The bag was heavy and full. He couldn't fit much more in except some single-serve Twinkies and Ho Hos by the front. He whistled to Greg and Sam, wherever they were.

"Goin' back to the truck."

Blake shoved his way out of the mangled exit, rubbing shoulders with women carrying baby formula and toilet paper and men with booze, kids circling around them. Greg staggered up ahead. He carried five twelve-packs of Coors with his back pockets stuffed with beef jerky. They dumped their booze into the truck bed.

"Where's Sam?" Blake asked.

"I thought he was with you."

Sam came running out moments later with radio cassette/CD player combos stacked in his arms. Blake remembered that they were on the back wall behind glass. A fresh cut bled on Sam's forearm.

"I hit a gold mine!" he said, tossing his loot in the truck bed.

"What you are going to do with all this cheap plastic shit?" Blake said. "Seems to me if we're stealing, it oughta be good stuff, right?"

The words had slipped out, but they looked at each other for a couple of exaggerated seconds, mutually acknowledging a desire to step up their criminal behavior a notch.

"I need a new amp," Greg said.

"A big-screen TV and VCR would be sweet," Sam said.

They headed south into Koreatown and smashed the window of a small music shop next to a liquor store that was being looted. There weren't any amplifiers, but they loaded up the bed with a bevy of instruments—acoustic guitars, violins, saxophones, and trumpets. Sam came out playing a freaking tuba.

"Haven't played this since high school."

Next they stopped at an electronics store. A crowd swarmed around a broken glass door. Kids and young men ducked through the jagged space and came back out with VCRs and boomboxes.

"Won't be able to get my rear projection through that hole like that," Sam said.

"Let's go around to the back," Blake said.

He drove down the alley, stopping at the loading dock. They busted the lock with the crowbar he kept under the seat for security and raised the garage door. All three of them caught their breath looking at cardboard boxes labeled Zenith, RCA, and Sony.

"Let's do this thing!" Sam shouted.

He spotted a forty-five-inch rear-projection Zenith in a box that could hold a family. They heaved, but it was impossible for them to lift. They opted for a twenty-six-inch Sony. The tuba was thrown out of the truck, and a thousand-dollar violin got crushed. Blake wanted to grab a car stereo with a removable faceplate to replace his stolen one, but a Honda screeched to a halt fifteen feet away. Four Asian men jumped out of the car. They looked slight, but the aluminum baseball bats and tire irons they carried did not.

"Hey you," a man in his forties with a thick accent said. "Put that back!"

"Oh, shit," Greg said.

"Let's go," Blake shouted.

The three of them piled into the truck. By the time Blake shoved the keys into the ignition and turned the engine over, a bat had smashed his driver's-side window, sending sharp projectiles all over them. A man opened the passenger-side door, but Sam punched him in the face before he brought his tire iron down. Another one tried to pull open the tailgate. Blake stomped on the gas. The man pitched forward, falling on his knees. The guy with the bat swung again, pounding the side of the F-150.

Blake heard gunshots as they raced down the alleyway. He looked into his rearview and saw one of the men firing a pistol.

They pulled over two blocks away and found that the TV was useless. Three bullets punctured the tube.

"I can't believe that fucker destroyed his own property," Sam said. "What an asshole."

Blake felt cheated too. Not only was the TV useless, most of the instruments were broken. All that risk for nothing. They tossed the TV onto the street, the tube shattering on the sidewalk.

"Where to next?" Sam asked, looking like a hungry wolf.

Blake read Greg's doubtful expression. "Let's head back home and be happy with the little bit we've got and thank the Lord we're still alive."

"Bullshit," Sam said, stomping on the only violin that wasn't damaged. "Just because some slant-eyes chased us down an alley doesn't mean we stop now. Hell no. Everybody else is takin' what they want. So should we."

"Suit yourself, but I ain't drivin' your sorry ass," Blake said.

They piled back into the truck without saying a word. Blake was happy to have Greg as a barrier between him and Sam. He wanted to smash Sam's head against the pavement and pound him senseless. His knuckles were white on the steering wheel as they headed up the nearly empty Western Avenue. They were close to home when he slammed on the brakes.

"What're you doing?" Greg asked.

Blake stared at the red couch in the window. The talisman to success beckoned him. Blake did a three-point turn and lined up the front bumper with the storefront window.

"Dude's lost his shit," Sam said, laughing.

"Buckle up, assholes," Blake said.

He slammed the gas, spinning his rear wheels, and then let off the brake. Sam screamed his rebel yell. The truck bounced over the sidewalk and crashed into the glass. Hard, translucent shards rained on the hood and cement.

Blake put the truck in reverse, turned it around, and backed the bed into the gaping hole of the store window. The rest of LA could burn and go to hell, but he was going to get what he was owed, dammit.

"Red leather couch first," Blake said.

The three of them scrambled out of the truck. Blake unhinged the tailgate and stepped inside, admiring the couch's beauty. Elegant leather, soft to the touch. His reward for time served.

"Come on now. I wanna get me a sweet Barcalounger," Sam said.

Sam and Greg hoisted the couch from the sides while Blake steadied it in the middle. They hadn't taken a step when Blake felt the air pressure in the store change. A bullet punctured the red leather couch, revealing white stuffing. Two Asian men—one young, the other older—stood in the back of the store aiming pistols. Greg and Sam dropped the couch on Blake's foot.

Blake dove behind the couch after the man's second shot. The bullet sliced the air by his arm. He looked at Sam and then Greg. Both had ducked behind furniture, guns in hand. Blake pulled his .22 from his waistband.

Another shot hit the couch.

Dammit, Blake thought. *Stop destroying my couch.*

"This is my business. My furniture." The man with a thick accent screamed, his voice breaking in anguish.

The couch took another round. Blake looked at Sam crouched behind a bed. He mouthed the words *On three*.

Blake turned to Greg, who nodded back.

"One," Sam mouthed, holding up a finger. "Two."

The next few seconds played out for what seemed like minutes and, later, an eternity. Crouching over the sofa, Blake pointed his .22 at the owner. He saw the young man, a long, lanky teenager, snap backwards. Sam had nailed him. Greg aimed at the owner, and splinters from a cabinet behind the man exploded. The owner's gun flashed bright orange. A bullet nipped the top of Blake's left ear. He returned the favor, squeezing the trigger, his sights centered on the man's body.

In the time that it took for the bullet to reach the man's chest, milliseconds really, it appeared to Blake that the owner became aware that his son had been shot. The hardened anger in his face softened to horror as his eyes shifted to where his son once stood. Then Blake's bullet plowed into him, and he fell backwards.

Blake thought he was going to puke. Greg and Sam grabbed him under the shoulders and pulled him into the truck. Blake glanced back at the space where the store-owners once stood. The emptiness seemed like a vast, burned-out canyon.

* * *

THEY DIDN'T SPEAK about it when they made it back home. They didn't say anything for almost two days. The TV always stayed on. Sam occasionally peeked out the window, .38 still in his hand, checking for prowlers. Greg sat in front of the TV, eyes puffy and red, shaking his head every now and then. Blake lay in his bed motionless, staring at the ceiling with a bottle of purloined Jack nearby. He kept replaying the expression on the man's face just before taking a bullet to the chest. It hit near the heart. He had to have died. Just the thought of that, killing another man over a piece of furniture, made Blake want to slam his head into a wall until there was nothing left above his neck.

How had he become this? Never in a million years would he have believed this could have happened. If rioters were going to break into his house, he'd be fine with it. They could tear him limb from limb. He wouldn't resist. Better than going to trial. He'd never be able to justify his crime to his family and friends.

Greg broke the silence on the third day.

"Guys, come here. You need to see this, now," he shouted.

Sam and Blake shuffled over to the TV. Greg turned up the volume. There was a police sketch of a long-haired guy that looked like Sam on the tube. The text labeled him as Shooter #1. Next was a drawing of Greg. The report mentioned he had red hair and fair complexion. Then there was a sketch of Blake. It wasn't accurate, but close enough. He was labeled Shooter #3. Then a hotline number appeared.

"That's supposed to be us?" Sam said with a scoff. "Of all the crazy shit goin' on out there, and they put pictures of us on the air? That there is reverse racism if I've ever seen it."

"The old man isn't dead," Greg said, looking at Blake.

Blake felt a wave of relief flood his body. "But his son?"

"Dead."

"'Cause I'm a better shot," Sam said, and then bit his lip. "Didn't mean it like that. But they had guns, and they were shootin' at us. It was justified."

"We broke in there, asshole," Blake said. He wanted to rip Sam's head off and punt it down the street. The fucking murderer.

"If they hadn't shot at us, we wouldn't've used our guns."

"You've been wantin' to kill somebody your entire life," Blake said, getting in Sam's face. "Especially somebody who's not white."

"That's a fuckin' lie. You're the asshole who broke into the place. You caused all this."

Blake shoved Sam against a wall. Sam bounced off and swung wide. They circled each other, fists clenched.

"Hey dipshits!" Greg shouted. "The Song family put a fifty-thousand-dollar bounty on our heads." Blake and Sam both turned to Greg. His skin had turned a pallid shade of green. "If y'all just stop and shut up, you would've heard it."

* * *

BLAKE TOOK SCISSORS to his hair that night, cutting off the rock star locks. Two days later, after the National Guard quelled the rioting by roaming the streets with their M-16s and military convoys, he drove his packed truck straight back to Oklahoma. He tossed his .22 into the Muddy Boggy Creek and grew a goatee that he never shaved off. Not even for his wedding with Charlotte Shaw, an old high school flame who still had a crush on him.

He wasn't in love. He just needed to be a new person. A different, better man. He took a job in shipping at a warehouse and answered to the name Hollywood. He'd tell stories about the rock stars he'd met, but didn't say anything about the riots except that it was crazy, and he knew it was time to get out of town. When anybody would ask about the nick on his ear, he'd say it was a wound from a bar fight.

One night Blake came home to find that Charlotte had bought a red futon for their guest room. Enraged, he threw the futon mat out into the front yard. She wanted to know why, but he couldn't tell her. That incident hastened the end of their already rocky marriage. Even the birth of their daughter, Meghan, couldn't keep them together.

Divorced with limited visitation rights, Blake developed a new set of habits. Singing karaoke like he was twenty, hooking up with available women, and drinking away the past as best he could. It wasn't much of a life, but it was a routine.

* * *

BLAKE WAKES UP with a start. Sunlight seeps through the window, and his head throbs like it was kicked with steel-toe boots. He turns to see his pistol lying on the bedside table. Staggering out of bed, he makes his way to the kitchen. He needs coffee and Tylenol by the handful.

He dumps the old grinds into the sink and pours what's left in the can into the coffee maker. Not much. Maybe two cups at best. He curses at himself for always running out of something when he needs it the most.

He fills the coffee pot with water, when something catches the corner of his eye. Something different. Turning, he sees Mr. Song sitting at his breakfast table. The glass pot shatters next to Blake's bare feet.

They stare at each other. Mr. Song is older. His hair is stark white, and scars line his face. His brown eyes, surrounded by wrinkles, are iron-hard. He holds a big, chrome revolver between his hands.

"It is a shame you broke the coffee pot. We cannot have coffee now."

"Yeah, cryin' shame," Blake says, looking at the shards lying by his feet. He can't believe he left his pistol in the other room.

"Come here and sit," Mr. Song says.

"Suppose I don't have much to say in this matter, do I?"

The man hints at a smile. "You suppose correct."

Blake walks with his hands in the air toward the table. The thought of running or flipping over the card table and punching the man in the face—what is he, at least sixty-five by now?—flashes and recedes in his mind. What would it matter? Blake is tired. Tired of hiding from his past, his moment of evil. If there is anybody in the world who has a right to judge him, a right to kill him, it is this man.

"Sit," Mr. Song says, motioning with the gun.

Blake pulls out a chair and sits, his elbows on the table. They look at each other for what seems like forever. Blake feels the scales of life and death being weighed.

"So you found me, Mr. Song," Blake says. "I want to apologize for . . . for that day. Though I know that means very little, I know. It was a crazy day, and I did horrible things. I am sorry that . . ."

Mr. Song holds up his hand, silencing Blake.

"Your apology is . . . not what I want."

A chill runs from Blake's scalp to his toes. He's certain

these are his final breaths on earth. All the wasted time he'd spent on worthless hedonistic pursuits and never enough quality moments with his daughter.

"I understand, sir. I guess, before you kill me, I'm glad I've had an opportunity to say sorry about what happened."

Mr. Song squeezes his eyes shut for a moment, as if holding back pain. "You know what I hate about you most?"

Blake has an idea, but he shakes his head. "No, sir."

"I hate that you could not shoot better."

"Excuse me?" Blake says, leaning in closer.

"I hate that you did not kill me in my store."

Blake blinks, trying to comprehend. "I . . . I don't understand."

"You are a father, yes?"

Blake nods, a lump growing in his throat. He tightens his fists. If Mr. Song even hints at threatening Meghan, Blake will throw himself across the table. Bullets be damned.

"If you killed me. If your gun was a bigger . . . caliber. Bigger than a twenty-two. Like this," he says, wagging what must be a .44. "If you aimed three centimeters lower, I would die. I would die and join my son in heaven." Mr. Song shook his head, holding back tears. "But no. My son died, and I lived. Nothing is worse. Do you understand?"

Blake nods, feeling sick. There is something worse than death. Survival. Mr. Song puts the revolver on the table and slides it toward him. Blake's first impulse is to grab it and shoot him. But he hesitates. It doesn't make sense. Is this a trap?

"What do you want me to do?" Blake says.

"I want you to finish the job. Kill me."

Mr. Song unbuttons his shirt and opens it. A long, pink scar runs across the frail man's concave chest. He points below the scar.

"Here. This is where I want you to shoot me."

"You can't be serious."

Mr. Song's eyes turn hard. "I live a dead life ever since the riots. I lost everything. Not just my son, but my family and everything I care about. I hated God for making me live. I hated him for letting you and your friends break into my store. I survived, but I could not look my wife and daughter in the face. My wife got sick, never left the bed. I drank, angry. Powerless. Police did nothing. I lost the business. Left my family. Every night I saw your face. Sam Boyle's face. Greg Duncan's face. I became hate. Hate became my mission. Ten years I spent looking. Finally last year, I found Greg in Baton Rouge. I remembered he shot at me wide. Hit a cabinet. He had big red hair, short now. All of you have short hair now. Greg apologized. Cried. I didn't care. Got the name of the man who killed my son. After he told me, I shot him dead. I felt nothing."

Blake catches his breath. Greg wasn't a bad guy at all. He didn't deserve to die like that.

"It wasn't easy to find Mr. Boyle," Mr. Song continues. "Took me five months. Small town in Tennessee. Small town like this. I was not so nice to him. He suffered. I was evil to him. He was a big man, overweight. He hated himself. For five days in an empty barn, I tried to make him feel the pain in his body that I feel in my soul." He shakes his head. "Useless. Stupid."

"He's dead too?" Blake asks, holding back the urge to vomit.

"Yes. He's with the devil now."

Blake looks at the gun on the table. It could be un-loaded. Maybe Mr. Song wants him to draw and click the chamber. A Korean test of character?

"So you found me next?" Blake says.

"Yes. But I didn't have satisfaction I wanted killing Mr. Boyle. I devoted my life to finding him. All of you. Now I feel . . . hollow. No joy. Killing did not satisfy. Vengeance is what I lived for, but now . . . If I kill you, I have no reason to live." He points his finger at Blake. "If you kill me, it will be made right. It should have happened then, in Los Angeles, but didn't."

"What if I don't kill you? I constantly have nightmares about that day. I don't know if I could survive knowing I killed you again."

"If you do not, I will kill your daughter, Meghan. She lives on 329 B Street with her mother."

Blake swipes the gun, pointing it at Mr. Song's head. He might spend the rest of his life in prison, but he will not allow his daughter to be murdered.

"Now you see what the loss of a child means."

The gun shakes in Blake's hand. It has become incredibly heavy.

"But . . . but what you want to do is wrong . . . what we did . . . what I did was a mistake. I didn't mean to shoot you or anybody. What you are talking about is intentional and . . . just evil, sir."

Mr. Song nods. "True. Wrong and evil. I became as bad as or worse than you. I deserve to be with the devil, not with my son in heaven. But I can't kill myself. You must do it." He grabs Blake's arm and points the barrel at his chest. "Do it, Mr. Henderson. You must. I cannot live any longer." He gives a look of pure, utter conviction.

Blake isn't sure how it happens, but his index finger tightens and a blast rings in his ears. Mr. Song bounces backwards, his head slamming against the back wall. A smile parts on his lips.

"Komapsumnida."

His eyes glaze over, lifeless. Blake looks down at the gun in his hand. He finally did it, killed the man he hadn't so many years earlier. This is so fucked up. What should he do now?

He hears a car pull up to his driveway and sees Angie getting out of her Camaro. No way is he facing her or anybody else today. Ever.

Blake raises the warm barrel to his temple. He can end this sordid saga right here in his kitchen. Los Angeles,

1992 in the furniture store on Western, and twenty-one years later, all of them dead. He just needs to pull the trigger.

"Not sure which way I'm headin'," he sings in a light whisper.

The Movement

THE WHITE-BLUE MOONLIGHT sinks behind the jagged silhouettes of redwoods that surround your hidden campsite. The sun won't rise for a couple more hours. Though the damp air is chilly, you don't notice. You know today is the day. You feel it in your bones. He will come. Even though his options are unlimited, you've obsessed over that prick long enough to predict his behavior. This journey you've been on, full of miscalculations, staggering heights, and ocean-bottom lows, will end today.

You're a wanted man. In a matter of weeks, you went from darling of the downtrodden to public enemy number one. It wasn't your first fall from grace either. Although you know this might be the final day of your life, you're okay with that. In your thirty-seven years, you've had more experiences than most people will have in a hundred.

However, thoughts of public perception and your legacy have been gnawing at you and keeping you awake. Nobody knows your true story: the reasons why and the unfiltered truth of it all. You've already published a few books, casting yourself as the whistleblower of the corrupt elite. But that is your alter ego, Jack Hamilton, the man who created The Movement and fought the corrupt powers. People should know the real you, Randall Waters, the one-time ambitious, misguided boy who metamorphosed into several incarnations before ending up as you are, a fugitive avenger.

All night you have been feverishly writing a memoir while staking out his compound. Eighty pages written in this composition notebook hold everything about you.

Written on the front and back pages are your life, your thoughts, your history. You flex your cramped fingers, dropping the rollerball pen on the redwood-needled carpet. Only one page left. You stare at the vast blankness of white. What will be your final words?

Reputations can change in an instant; that is why, if you die today, this manuscript must survive. You've been demonized and praised. Now you've given the reasons for your actions, documenting the why so people will understand. You just hope the manuscript will be revered like Julius Caesar's campaign notes, and not reviled and dismissed like John Wilkes Booth's diary.

* * *

My Life as a Scoundrel and a Savior
By Randall Waters aka Jack Hamilton

I was born Randall Eugene Waters in Goldspar, Arizona. My father worked as a maintenance man for the school district while my mother raised seven children. I was second to last. My brothers and sisters fit perfectly with the school and the town. The boys devolved from jocks to blue-collar, beer-bellied couch jockeys. The girls transformed from cheerleaders to baby machines. I had nieces and nephews who were only a couple of years younger than me. I knew early that I didn't belong. I was the runt with brains, and I wanted out of that squalid, backwards town.

My grades and test scores were good enough for any of the Ivy League schools. I even got scholarships, but my parents, who didn't have a dime of savings and never gave a positive thought to education, couldn't afford to send me East. I had to settle for a state school where I became the big fish, even with thirty thousand students. President's Honor Roll, Phi Beta Kappa, and all the awards in between without breaking a sweat. I majored in Finance because it dealt with the one thing I never had: money.

The first time I met Jeffrey Donahue IV was during our internship at World Trust Bank. That was my only shot to get the future job I wanted, and we were forty of America's brightest college juniors vying for two positions the following year. I scraped by on the less-than-minimum-wage salary eating the meager snacks in the lounge, often working close to sixteen hours so that nobody could even come close to the volume of work I generated.

Jeffrey, this tall, blond, and blue-eyed Aryan's wet dream, seemed to do no work at all. He walked around the offices like he owned the place, joking with men and flirting with women. Soon they were gloating about the bars and parties from the previous night. I ignored it all and crunched numbers, knowing there was no way in hell Jeffrey would make it.

Yet, the next summer, the two of us, fresh graduates, entered the executive program. I wore the same suit as the year before, but Jeffrey didn't. And every day following it seemed like he wore a different tailor-made suit for three weeks solid. I couldn't understand how he, of all people, had made the cut. Jeffrey had done the least amount of work of any intern. True, he went to Princeton and his grandfather or somebody had been Treasury Secretary in the Eisenhower administration, but I doubted if he could even carry a remainder on a simple N648 form.

I hated his very existence. As before, wanting to differentiate myself, I immediately dove into work, creating extra analyses and reports on trends that weren't required. My hard work was always praised, but Jeffrey, the social butterfly, kept joking with the execs and went to parties even veteran employees were never invited to. I kept my distance from him, but he approached me one day.

"Hey, Randy."

"Randall."

I remember him rolling his eyes. "Sure. I realize we've been working here for the same amount of time and I don't know you. We should get a drink tonight."

"No, too busy. I promised Mr. Wynn a report on—"

"Don't worry about Max. He can wait. Seriously, tonight at six I'm taking you out of here. They don't pay you enough to see the janitors." He slapped me on the shoulder causing me to pitch forward as he gave off his goddamn winning smile.

Though I tried to resist his charm, the rich prick won me over. Max . . . Mr. Wynn's report could wait. Over a few rounds of Scotch, Jeffrey outlined banking and finance in a way I'd never heard before. "We don't need people in banking, they need us," he said. I tried to argue how asinine that statement was, but he held up a hand. I still remember his speech, delivered with utter confidence and contempt.

"People make lousy livings doing shitty jobs. They choose to do that, right? This is America, you can choose what you want to be, so if you choose to be a poor schmuck and be stupid with your money, then fuck you. I'll take your savings, and if don't have any, I'll lend you money as long as you keep on paying it back to me with interest, biatch. Banking is a numbers game. If you have all wealthy clients, you'll get rich, but they'll count every goddamned penny that comes and goes. Not the masses, though. They have stuff like Friends, NFL playoffs, and PTAs to worry about. Take a little here and there, they'll never notice. Of course we need numbers, a lot of them since we'd only take a quarter of a cent to the dollar, but it'll work. They'll never notice."

I was astounded. Ripping off the working class, people like my family, and insulting them on top of it. But he had said something even more important to the hyper-ambitious person I was then. "You said we?"

He threw his arm around me, embedding a cufflink into my shoulder. "I've got the plan, and you've got the number-crunching skills. What do you say?"

"We'll do this at Greater American?"

"No, we start our own bank. I can get the capital, but you come up with the business model. We'll stay here for a few more years, building up connections, and then strike

out on our own. I'll be the president, you'll be the CEO. Are you in?"

Perhaps it was the three glasses of Scotch burning through my body, but I said yes. A CEO before thirty, how could I not?

* * *

"THE SKUNK HAS landed," a voice crackles over the walkie-talkie by your knee.

Your pulse quickens. Skunk: the code word for Jeffrey. The man you planted at the Santa Rosa airport two years ago has finally paid off.

"Ready on positions," you speak softly into the wireless. The message travels out to the remnants of your crew, the last fragments of The Movement.

Oren is at the back of the property. An Iraq veteran demolition expert who lost his house and eventually his wife and kids, he is full of anger with nothing to lose. You've given him direction to tunnel that aggression.

Greg is at the bottom of the hill behind a large coyote brush shrub, watching the massive steel gate at the front of the compound fifty yards away. A sweet country boy looking for a family, he found you, and you accepted him. Of everybody remaining, you feel the most responsible for him, wishing he had deserted you like others had.

Cam, your right hand and lieutenant, is east of the hill with a view of Russian River Road. You see yourself in him, the same energy and ambition. You feel like you know him thoroughly. If it weren't for him, you'd be dead, and this final strike wouldn't be possible. His loyalty is unmatched.

Inside the compound is a security guard named Murray. You've never met him, but Cam says he's solid. He's in on the plan. If he were a snitch, you'd be caught by now.

You stand, stretching your taut muscles and trying to relieve the ache of hunching over a notebook on hard ground all night. Walking to the edge of the hill, you check the chamber of your Beretta and blow into it, making sure nothing is lodged inside. The sky is gray, the stars fading away like mist. Looking down across the road, you see lights from the compound below. You taste the bitterness of disgust from the back of your throat as memories flood through your body, recalling your first visit there.

* * *

Jeffrey's family has owned a northern California estate for a couple of generations. Known as a retreat from the eyes of the world, powerbrokers traveled there to relax and plan the fate of the world. For many of the exclusive guests, it was the stop before or after the drunken orgy at the Bohemian Grove. Mostly finance executives and congressmen on important committees made annual visits to the compound, where brandy and red wine flowed freely.

I was summoned there to meet Jeffrey's father and a few of his cronies almost a year after those first drinks with him. I had slaved away at my home computer, creating the master document for a new mega-bank, generating dozens of models that yielded the highest growth and accumulation of assets in the shortest amount of time. I had marked all the policies and regulations that might hinder progress and then provided workaround solutions, noting that legal advice should be sought first. This was my magnum opus, eight hundred pages detailing a truly streamlined, powerful bank that could grow exponentially and create wealth faster than any other financial institution ever had.

A week after I finished the manifesto, they flew me out on a private jet from New York to Santa Rosa's tiny airport. A limo escorted me to the compound. Back then there was only a small remote-controlled gate at the entrance. The limo motored up a paved road to an enormous house that looked more like a university library. Redwoods surrounded the massive house, but the three-story marble columns in front seemed almost as large. A quote from

TRAVIS RICHARDSON

Adam Smith was etched in wood above heavy lacquered doors: All money is a matter of belief.

The interior was even more ostentatious. Antique furniture and enormous oil paintings of European hunters on horseback littered a cavernous entry.

"In here!" a voice shouted from a room on the left.

I walked into a room covered from floor to ceiling in dark wood paneling. Tree-sized logs burned in a fireplace as large as a compact car. Mica lamps added to the sinister orange glow on the faces of white haired men sitting on leather couches, holding brandy snifters, and looking at me in flickering shadows.

"Randall, the man of the hour," Jeffrey said, jumping up from a couch. His perfectly aligned teeth set in a wide smile, he threw an arm around me. "I want you to meet the board."

I had never been in a fraternity. Because of either my financial background or less-than-pedigreed looks, I had been declined in two rushes. In front of me sat men of consequential power that any one of those frat hacks at my state school would have given a testicle to meet. They smiled at me, approving. My body shook with nervous and excited energy. If I could impress these power-brokering geezers, I would reap the vast amounts of money I had dreamed of.

Three days of intense debate, study, brandy-laced coffees, and Cuban cigars later, I received the nomination and accepted the position of Vice President of the Home Equity Division of the yet to be formed Statesmen Bank and Trust. A few of the old coots would sit on the board, Jeffrey's father would be the CEO, and Jeffrey would be the Chief Operations Officer.

"Honestly, Randall," Jeffery Donahue III said. "You are a nobody. Financial genius, yes. A known player in banking, no. We need to build trust from investors over the next few years. If you bring in the money and assets that you say you can in the housing-loan area, you will be in line for CFO and then CEO after that."

The group infused close to $80 million. Like the Silicon Valley tech companies, we were a startup. For the first time in my life, I was on the cutting edge.

Jeffrey had spent some time with me while I worked like crazy on the proposal. Small stuff like having food delivered to my apartment or taking me out for a drink when I finished a section. But after the powerbrokers approved Statesmen Bank, we had dinner almost every night. He took me out shopping to improve my look and confidence. He taught me how to tie the Windsor knot, how to match variations of beige, the fine difference between a good and an excellent tailor. He also taught me how to talk to women with a confidence bordering on arrogance and condescension, and then leave coldly in the morning so there are no mixed messages. For once in my lonely life, I felt like I had a real friend.

My division, home loans and equity, pulled in the most money. The variable interest rate locked customers into a forever-changing percentage that I controlled. If they defaulted, Statesmen would own the asset, able to foreclose and resell the property. It worked very well for the bank's portfolio, and I heard chatter from the board that I might leapfrog to the CEO job when Jeffrey III stepped down.

I met Katrina, a blonde, surgically enhanced woman who did things I didn't know were physically possible. I spent a fortune on her needs. Like Jeffrey, I now had a month's worth of Italian tailored suits. I bought a penthouse condo in Manhattan and a beach house in Cape Cod. I felt like Superman, totally invincible. It seemed nothing could stop me.

Then there was a sudden downturn in the housing market, and all of those houses Statesmen Bank owned lost their value almost overnight. It wasn't a snowball, but an avalanche of bad and worse news. Suddenly the majority of customers defaulted on their loans within a couple of months, and I was stuck with a glut of unsellable McMansions in shitty areas of the country. The board put pressure on me to stop the bleeding, as the bank had lent millions to customers who were abandoning their houses. I changed the variable rates to lower fixed ones, but they still couldn't make the payments. When I kicked the defaulters out, the homes were trashed with the appliances and copper piping torn out. Planned neighborhoods became ghost towns with squatters taking up residence and weeds growing waist-high in the yard.

It was around that time that Jeffrey stopped coming into the office. He gave half-hearted excuses at first and then nothing. He didn't return calls or email. The board also fell suspiciously quiet. It was unnerving.

I remember heading to work on a Monday with a massive hangover. I had split up with Katrina after a vicious argument on Friday night and then spent the weekend on a bender. It wasn't because of her that I drank myself stupid. There were several banks in trouble, and the entire country was swirling down the crapper. The sense of doom was overwhelming.

When I arrived at the office, it was eerily empty. Just the receptionist and a handful of assistants. We wondered aloud if we missed a holiday. I sat at my computer and found that I was locked out. Before I could make a call to Jeffrey or the IT department, SEC and FBI agents swarmed into the offices. They led me out in handcuffs, reading the Miranda.

* * *

"SKUNK IS COMING from the east," Cam says over the air.

The gray sky melts into hints of blue. Holding up your binoculars, you watch the shadowy outline of the road. It feels like it takes hours, but seconds later a pair of headlights punctures the darkness below. The outline of a Lincoln limousine emerges. It is Jeffrey. You're sure of it. You shiver, feeling excitement. Revenge—no, justice—can finally be exacted. The car turns at the gate, stops for a brief moment while it opens, and then rolls up to the estate. Three men get out. One has Jeffrey's shape, and the other two are built like linebackers. You know it is Jeffrey. It has to be, but the distance is too far and it's too dark to be certain.

You can't be wrong. The FBI and most Americans think you are in Mexico. You gave your cell phone and a credit card to a follower with a similar build. He is supposed to use one or the other every couple of days in different towns. It seems to be working. A thought crosses your mind. Maybe Jeffrey has a body double. You stifle a laugh, but acknowledge a little paranoia is prudent.

"Are we ready?" Greg asks over the radio. His voice has a nervous quiver.

"Hold your positions," you say softly. "We need confirmation from inside. We can only blow our wad once."

* * *

I remember sitting in the courtroom as a parade of wealthy liars and a few impoverished souls testified against me. I had done bad things, I admit that now, but I did not act alone. The board members lined up one by one to say that they were shocked and horrified when they "found out" what I was doing. These were the same bastards that had praised me and, like starving dogs, begged for more money. Even my secretary testified against me, making me look like a lecherous ogre by twisting our causal daily banter into harassment.

The deepest cut came from Jeffrey. Immaculately dressed, he put his hand on the Bible with an expression of absolute solemnity. The holy book should have seared his hand, but he held it there, vowed to tell the truth, and then stared at me, squinting his eyes with intense reproach. I realized then that I did not have a single friend in the world, and I felt the ground sink from under me. Reversing the facts of our first meeting, he said I pushed him to use his family connections to start up a new lending organization. I was flabbergasted. A brazen lie, told so coolly and confidently. I lost it. My body shook, and I saw only red. I remember shouting and running toward that son of a bitch, and then the world went black.

The next thing I remembered was waking up in a hospital handcuffed to a bed, my head throbbing. My attorney, Sherman, was there. Nobody else. He told me I was Tased by a deputy and then fell forward, hitting my head against the bench. Sherman wanted to settle immediately. I didn't. I wanted to tell my side. The truth of what really happened. He shook his head like I was a child.

"Too late. You look like a crazed lunatic to the jury. Maybe on appeal."

I was furious. I settled for ten years in federal prison. I hated everyone and everything, but I hated Jeffrey the most.

* * *

AN UNFAMILIAR VOICE murmurs, "Skunk." It must be Murray's. Jeffrey is indeed inside. Wrapping the memoir in plastic, you shove it behind your bulletproof vest. You check the Beretta on your side and the pistol on your ankle holster. They're both there. You reach into your supply bag and take out a grenade and a smoke bomb, stuffing them into your jacket pockets.

"Move to position B," you call out on the walkie-talkie.

Using the contours of the land, you run from bush to tree to boulder. The weight of heavy boots and equipment, plus the ache of bones and joints, do not bother you. You are at the end. A clear light shines at the end of a tunnel.

You sidle next to Greg. He smiles warmly, but his eyes are bulging in excitement. He looks like he is fifteen.

"We're really going to do this, aren't we?"

You nod and want to tell him he can stay behind. But you both hear crunching undergrowth and turn to the gully a few yards away. Cam, in full camo, crawls over to you. Twigs and bits of leaves hang from his curly hair. He smells rancid, probably as bad as you do.

"Oren has the explosives in place, sir."

You never like it when he calls you sir, but he was in the army. Habits can be hard to break. You know he'll be a cornerstone once you rebuild The Movement, which will be even stronger with today's victory.

"Great," you say. "When the gate opens, we'll get into the second location, then we'll detonate and breach."

Cam nods. He has an uneasy smile.

"It'll be all right," you whisper with a light slap on his shoulder. "This will be over in a few minutes. I know this place."

* * *

My first year in the federal penitentiary was the worst. It's not as horrific as movies make it look. Maybe it is for violent offenders, but I wouldn't know. I was with mostly white-collar criminals and a few bank robbers. In those initial weeks I felt I could have torn the head off of any convict there. Not that I had much physical clout, but intense anger seethed through my body. It was centered on Jeffrey Donahue.

To me, he was the sole reason I was locked up, but I was willing to take it out on anybody who upset me. Oscar, my undersized ex-bank-robbing cellmate, took a lot of abuse. It got to the point that the fifty-year-old flinched anytime I moved.

Around my second year, I decided to channel all of that anger into a tell-all book about the Statesmen Bank. I worked on it for over thirteen months, fact-checked as much as I could from the prison library, and finally com-posed a detailed, seven-hundred-page account. I was shocked to find that nobody wanted it. Only three years into my imprisonment, and the scandal was old news.

When a small press asked to buy it, I was more than happy to sign over all my rights and give the fact-checkers my entire research. I found out later it had all been a ruse. The publisher had been purchased by Statesmen, and the contract I signed prohibited me from writing anything else about the bank.

I cannot explain the fury and impotence I felt. I had been totally outflanked for the second time by these bastards. To add more insult to injury, Jeffrey oversaw the publishing house's operations. That slimy, blue-blooded weasel. I vowed to do many horrific and painful things to him when I got out, but I still had over six years to go.

Then, I found Jesus . . . and Mohammad too.

What I really found was the power of faith and devotion. I watched different charismatic leaders in the prison chapel and on TV preaching from a single book with devoted disciples following every word to fortify themselves with inner strength, satisfaction, and hope. There was a lot of repetition, and evidence of God came from the gut. Verifiable proof was not necessary . . . or even possible. The emotion of faith, however, made God real. There were very few, if any, grays. Every decision in life was black or white: you either made the righteous choice or committed sin. And evil had a leader: the ultimate boogey man, Satan. He was the one who caused humanity's misfortunes. Like talk-radio jockeys who blast liberals for every problem happening in the world, I knew I could crush Jeffrey and the Statesmen Bank with these tactics.

I found a role model in Saul of Tarsus. A tireless persecutor of early Christians, he later became the biggest evangelist for their cause. He just changed his name to Paul and said Jesus spoke to him.

The name change was easy. I hated the name Randall Waters. I took Jack Hamilton as a handle, the masculine name I never had. To transform like the Apostle Paul, I needed to be blinded by Jesus. That would be difficult. Then it hit me. Reform. That's what every prisoner is supposed to do in the clink, right? I didn't need to go to Antioch. I could have a spiritual epiphany behind the bars.

The first person I needed to win over was my cellmate. We hadn't spoken in years. I remember our conversation vividly.

"Don't you think it's wrong—" I started one night in my bunk.

"You talkin' to me?" he said.

"Who else is in here?"

"I don't want to hear it. Especially if it's from you."

"Is that so? You just enjoying sitting in this cell here, biding your time . . . decaying into dust?"

"What kind of dumbshit question is that, stupid bank man?"

I knew that if I could win over Oscar, I would convert others. I jumped down from the bunk. He flinched.

"Why did you call me a bank man?" I asked.

"Say what?"

"A bank man. Do I look like I'm working in a bank?"

"You're nuts, man."

"I used to work at a bank. I used to sell reverse mortgages and variable interest loans intended to skyrocket. I used to, but no longer. I'm in prison, and I'm reformed."

"Yeah, we all are in here. You ain't so special."

"I'm only special in that I've seen the light. The light of change. The light that says not only do I need to change my ways, but I must expose those who do as I once did."

I gazed at Oscar, wide-eyed. Crazy. Like I meant it. Oscar tried to hold my stare but finally dropped his head.

"Whatever you say, man."

I knew I had him. It might take a few weeks of harassing indoctrination, but he was listening. So I gave him the hard sell. "What I'm trying to say is that you put in the time for the crime, and yet there are so many people out there that haven't. They are CEOs running banks. They don't lift wallets; they steal millions of dollars of hard earned money from thousands of honest people. They enjoy the good life and have political protection. Doesn't that get you mad?"

Oscar looked up, eyes blazing. "Of course it does. But there ain't a damn thing we can do about it. You know that. So shut the hell up."

I shook my head. "No, there is. We need to expose those motherfuckers and take back what they've taken from the people."

"And how do you plan to do that?"

"We're going to start a movement."

"We?"

I slapped Oscar on the shoulder and jumped to the top

bunk. *"Sleep tight, partner."*

I kept after Oscar for two weeks until we started discussing inequities and the best ways to bring awareness to the masses. By the end of the month, he was my first believer. I started going around the prison yard asking other prisoners the same questions. "Have you served your time to society?" "What do you think about the white-collar criminals who make millions illegally and are untouchable?" "Isn't it time to do something about it?" They gave me skeptical looks and shook their heads, but I could tell they were listening. I kept at it. Soon they were talking back to me, saying they were powerless. I countered. They weren't powerless as a whole, only as individuals. Even prison guards leaned in closer, and I noticed barely perceptible nods.

Organized meetings came next. Oscar arranged them, and each one was larger than the next. Locations varied around the prison yard, and we would break whenever a guard walked by. But then I talked to the guards, and they too had been screwed by the banking fiasco. Eventually they allowed me to preach to the prisoners unabated and often stood around the periphery to listen in. Every word I said was a black-and-white statement with absolute confidence. "The people should rule, not the privileged few." In the winter I moved into the recreation room, but it was not large enough. The warden allowed for morning, afternoon, and evening services in the cafeteria as long as the guards monitored me.

Prisoners told their relatives on the outside. There was no official name for what I'd organized, just The Movement. Since I didn't have computer access, I wrote daily memos that were taken outside and posted on a blog. I wrote under my new identity, Jack Hamilton. The blog went from a couple of dozen views to hundreds and then hundreds of thousands.

I also contacted those whose lives I had ruined. I started with the toughest one of all, Mrs. Stella January. Her testimony had been damming.

She and her retired husband had mortgaged their paid-off house for a loan at a variable rate. The interest rate shot up a few months later, and the Januarys burned through their life savings and refinanced again, only to default and hand the house over to Statesmen. Mr. January put a bullet in his head, and his wife lived out of a car. I remember feeling the sharp arrows from the jurors' eyes.

It took seven letters before she responded, telling me to stop writing and rot in hell. I kept writing her, giving her a journal of my transformation, telling her my need to make amends and to avenge against "those who have cheated the poor and have not paid the justice they owe."

Eventually she wrote back, forgiving me and encouraging me to expose "those just like you." I wrote other victims from my banking days, and soon dozens of victims who had lined up to prosecute me asked how they could join my movement.

* * *

"IN TEN," MURRAY'S voice comes over the walkie-talkie, and ten seconds later the gate opens.

You, Greg, and Cam haul ass, sprinting across the road and through the gate. It is about fifty yards up the road to the compound, but you don't need to get that far. There is a giant rose garden to the left of the mansion, planted by Jeffrey's grandmother or somebody. You just need to get there without anybody seeing you. You were out of breath several steps ago; your lungs cry out in pain.

"Oh shit. Somebody's coming out," Greg says from behind you.

You look at the enormous front door pushing open. You're less than twenty feet from cover. A bodyguard steps out. He looks like a steroid-using ultimate fighter. You slide on the wet grass into the cover of the rose bushes. Cam and Greg fall beside you.

Anemic orange rays glimmer in the distance, but gray is still dominant. Peering through the bushes, you see the guard look your way, but then he scans the property in the other direction and walks to the car. He grabs a duffel bag from the driver's seat and strides back inside the house.

You finally breathe. "That was close," Greg says. Both you and Cam nod. At any minute, Murray will walk out with the bodyguards. That will be the signal. Absolutely no return. You remember your memoir. You feel panicked. You might not make it out alive; it needs to be found. You pull out the plastic-encased notebook from your vest and stare at it. Between those black-and-white marbled covers you're leaving the world an explanation for your actions, ridding incorrect speculations. Is it enough? You remember the last blank page, take out your pen and start writing.

"What's that?" Greg whispers.

"It's my memoir," you say trying to figure a tone between reverence and hokiness. You write a few more sentences, but grow frustrated because you can't seem to find the words for what you want to say. Murray is going to step out any minute, and you're blanking under the pressure cooker of time. You dash a couple more lines and sign your name at the bottom. You rewrap the notebook, place it under a white rose bush, and cover it with dirt. You turn to your brothers-in-arms.

"If I don't make it out of here alive, I want one of you to take the notebook and put my words online."

"You're not going to die . . ." Greg starts.

"I'll grab it, sir," Cam says. Cam's eyes are directly on you, looking wholeheartedly sincere.

"Thanks," you say. "We'll see if we're dead or alive in just a few minutes."

* * *

When a major publishing house asked me to write a book based on my blog, I was skeptical. I wasn't going to get fooled again. So I asked an Oakland press known for more radical and controversial texts if they would be interested. They were, and they sold my first book,

Scoundrels, and then the call-to-arms follow up, *When Scoundrels Attack: How to Stop and Defeat Those Greedy Bastards*, by the boatloads.

I knew I had made a national impact with The Movement, but nothing prepared me for the day I stepped out of prison. There were hundreds, maybe a thousand people waiting for me. The banners, the cheers, it was overwhelming. It is one thing to write letters of support, but to show up in person to fucking Nowhere, Kansas. Wow. I knew I had created something powerful that could crush Jeffrey and his ilk.

In my first months with internet access, I worked furiously to expose all of those who exploited the masses. I listed the home addresses of CEOs from most banks and every credit card company. I used social media to organize protests in New York outside of the Stock Exchange and various banking headquarters, in DC outside of the Capitol and the Treasury, and a few in northern California outside of the Bohemian Club and the Donahue compound. I kept blogging and uploaded YouTube videos every few days. I was offered TV shows but declined. I wasn't going to have anybody dictate what I could do.

I quickly found my success created problems, not only with the elite powers who threw lawsuits at me daily, but also with my followers. Using royalties from my books, I rented a spacious Spanish colonial in Pasadena, where I could absorb three hundred days a year of the sunshine that I been denied in prison. Not long after moving in, followers began showing up on my doorstep. Like the Joads, they had lost everything and had packed their cars with their remaining possessions. They wanted me to provide a solution. I was their last hope.

I employed the first few families with jobs like research and organizing rallies. But as more arrived in campers and jalopies, my well-heeled neighbors used the city council and police to fine and pressure me. I had a moment of deep reflection.

Being a leader of the poor is not easy, and I questioned

why I had traveled this path. The Movement provided an outlet for my vengeance. It was personal for me, but it was also personal for all of the members of The Movement too. I had gone to jail, but they had lost a lot more and were slaves to credit cards with high compounding interest. We had all been screwed, but they needed my voice. I felt I couldn't let them down, but I didn't have a quick solution to provide for my supporters. Then it came from an unlikely source.

Mrs. Victoria Winston was the widow of the late billion-aire Harold Winston, who had manipulated California's energy crisis in the nineties, causing record-high electricity bills, bankrupting thousands, and even causing deaths. I cited that deceased scoundrel in both of my books and condemned his family for living luxuriously off of ill-gotten gains. Guilt-ridden by my prose, she had heard of my housing dilemma—exploited by the media—and gave me a thousand acres of land along with a ranch house in west Texas. Although I was apprehensive about moving to the Longhorn State, it was the only option.

Once on that flat and dusty land, even more flocked to me. The ranch turned into a commune. I kept the new-comers busy tending cattle and planting acres of crops. The older ones had cafeteria or infirmary jobs. If they didn't work, they were kicked out. I wasn't giving handouts, I was building a self-sufficient organization.

I continued to write and send out weekly videos, but this time in front of an audience. As The Movement kept growing, we accepted donations and obtained nonprofit status.

Since leaving prison, I had kept tabs on Jeffrey. He sat on several banking boards, but was not the head of anything: powerful but never public. His wealth had accumulated tremendously. I had him watched day and night.

I developed a circle of capable men and women. The guilt-ridden corporate types were sent back to financial institutions as spies, while those with military and police training were given surveillance and security duties. Like the National Guard, the latter group held a one-weekend-a-month paramilitary training on a remote part of the property. I wasn't looking to start any violence, but since I had provoked the powerful, I wanted to be ready if "something" happened.

A chain of command was developed to take care of all the operations. A young man named Cameron "Cam" Jennings stood out, and became my Chief Operations Officer. He was an ambitious ex-army man with a degree in Business Management. He always looked to expand and strengthen The Movement.

When Oscar, my former cellmate, was released, I hired him as my personal secretary. He had kept The Movement thriving in the prison after I left. He transitioned quickly to the commune after twenty-seven years in lockup and kept me organized.

From the beginning, Cam and Oscar didn't get along. Oscar didn't trust Cam, and Cam thought the ex-con was too old and had institutional syndrome. I thought a little disagreement was healthy, like the way Washington had Jefferson and Hamilton bickering on the same cabinet. Cam pushed for expansion, while Oscar always voiced caution. Sometimes the atmosphere was tense, but I believed it made us stronger.

Things ran smoothly for a couple of years until the infamous Bloody Monday. I decided to commemorate the anniversary of the start of the Great Depression on the last Monday of October by holding a rally in the morning and then marching over to the New York Stock Exchange in the afternoon. We had permits for Union Park, but the march was held under wraps.

Busloads of the discontented came from far and wide. More than I had imagined, at least a couple hundred thousand. Populists and musicians took the stage and belted out their sentiments about the capitalist crooks. I finished the mid-afternoon with graphs of inequities displayed on a thirty-foot screen, along with pictures of the *ultra-wealthy who made capital by exploitation. The crowd was whipped into an angry frenzy. I mentioned that Wall Street was a few miles away. "What should we do? How about we go there before the closing bell and let the goons of greed know we, the people, are watching them? Does this sound like a good idea?" The shouts of approval were tremendous.*

But before the crowd made the two-mile hike down Broadway, thousands of NYPD and the National Guard had cut off several square blocks leading to the Exchange. There were too many assembled in an hour. Somebody in my organization had tipped somebody off. I had no idea who.

Tens of thousands of my supporters marched up to the blocked streets from all directions, unable to meet in front of the Stock Exchange as planned. The scene was chaotic. The police waved batons and shotguns shouting at us to disperse immediately. My people, pressed shoulder-to-shoulder and packed dozens of bodies deep, were infuriated at being denied their First Amendment right of assembly. Then, all at once, assholes troublemakers that weren't with us tore through the crowd, taunting the authorities by throwing bottles and trash at them. Although they wore anarchy-circled As and covered their faces with black bandanas, they seemed wrong, inauthentic. (I've always had zero tolerance for anarchists, having them thrown out at events.) These guys looked like they bathed regularly, and their uniforms were creased as if unpacked an hour earlier.

More and more people kept arriving, compounding the insanity of the situation. I remember yelling at the top of my voice, trying to keep order, when somebody called my name: my given one, Randall. I turned, and Oscar leapt in front of me. There were gunshots, and Oscar slumped.

I caught him before he fell. Around me was mayhem— screaming and shoving. A middle-aged man wearing a faded American flag T-shirt with some cable pundit's slogan pointed a revolver at me, glaring with all the hate in the world. Suddenly, Cam grabbed the man from behind and threw him head-first into the pavement. Blood oozed from the man's unconscious face. There were more gunshots, and hundreds of panicked people stampeded.

I pulled Oscar along with the crowd. He bled horribly. I needed to get my friend to the hospital, but I was caught in a current of staggering bodies and swinging elbows. I kept dragging Oscar, pushed by the mass of bodies away from Wall Street.

Finally I found refuge in an alley. I tried to stop the bleeding, but it was too late. Oscar, dying in my arms, said that The Movement was worth dying for and warned me to watch my back. I sobbed mightily.

The police arrested me and another six hundred. They charged me with inciting a riot and were trying to make a homicide case too. Thirteen had died, including an officer, and thousands were injured. Windows of buildings in a three-mile radius had been smashed, and cars had been overturned and razed. The media ramped up a smear campaign against me.

I never found out who killed Oscar and attempted to assassinate me. Cam, who was also arrested, said the man had been trampled seconds after he hit the ground. There were so many who would love to see me dead. Many powerful people wanted the populace to be sedate again. The shooter looked like a disciple of the airwave sleaze, but maybe they wanted me to think that.

There was another problem. I had traitors in The Movement, but who? The entire riot had been a setup. The police had been aware of the march the entire time and kept quiet, never contacting us. The hooligans weren't mine either. When thinking of powerful people who could manipulate a peaceful demonstration into a riot, I thought of the board.

After making bail, I returned to Texas knowing I needed to retaliate, fast and hard. I was definitely going to serve jail time again and expected the FBI to shut down the commune within a week. The powers that had Oscar killed *were trying to eliminate me and discredit The Movement. It was payback time.*

I had prepared for violent responses since the beginning of The Movement, but only as a last resort. I wrote up a hit list and sent out a message to all of the operators to take out the trash. Five days later, in a single night, seven national execs and, in one unfortunate case, an entire family were terminated. Most were taken out with bombs, but bullets were also used. Many more properties and buildings were destroyed, including all of Jeffrey's real estate, except for the compound which had been fortified after the first protests years earlier. Every Statesmen board member was executed, besides Jeffrey . . . because I wanted it that way.

A dozen of my elite staff escaped the compound before the FBI raid. We expected it and were gone hours after "The Night of Justified Vengeance." I felt bad leaving my followers behind to fend off the Feds, but time was of the essence. I had to finish this before I got caught. I had to get Jeffrey Donahue.

My staff rendezvoused in a small town in New Mexico four days later. We came up with a plan and split up. One group went to Mexico as a decoy, and another to Michigan to talk to the militias. My group, composed of Greg, Oren, and Cam, headed west. Only Cam knows my true plan. He understands that Jeffrey was the cause of all of this bloodshed and nonsense.

* * *

MURRAY WALKS OUT the door with the other guards. He lights a cigarette. That's the sign. Cam radios Oren on the other side of the property.

"Showtime." A moment later Oren's voice saws over the wireless, "In five." Four. Three. Two. One. Boom! The ground shakes like an earthquake. Murray points behind the mansion, where smoke billows into the rising orange sun. He yells to the muscleheads, who run to the back of the property. You sprint to the front door, Cam and Greg behind you. Murray waits.

"Skunk's in the poolroom," he says as you pass him.

You know this room, having played snooker with some of this century's great financial scoundrels. Men whose names the public never sees, because they want it that way, and yet their impact is global. Many of their names appeared in obituaries two weeks ago.

Cam and Greg follow you through an elaborate hallway and down the stairs. You feel excitement. The end is now. Jeffrey is your obligation. You could have had him assassinated, but you preached personal responsibility. You're walking the walk. You smile, thinking about life drifting out of those cornflower-blue eyes.

You hear your men's footsteps on the basement stairs behind you and stop. The poolroom door is shut, but light floods around the bottom of the door. This is where Jeffrey is—this is where generations of financial malfeasance will end, where you will be avenged.

When you kick open the door, you notice the missing pool tables. It doesn't make sense. You run across the empty expanse to the smoking room, renowned for its walk-in humidor, Beretta raised. Greg hustles to your side, and Cam is behind you. You inhale the slightest scent of cigar smoke, but reaching for the door you find it locked. Bam! A deafening blast.

The door, the adjacent wall, your hands, and your face are covered in warm, red gunk and grayish matter. Greg's brains. You watch your loyal comrade slide from the wall to the floor, the front of his young face missing. Immediately, from the base of your stomach, nausea shoots upward. You know you've been set up ... again. Is it Murray?

Gripping the Beretta, you swivel and duck, aiming at the entry door. You're going to die, but not before squeezing off a few rounds. You fire into an empty doorway until your gun clicks empty. It is only then that you notice Cam is standing over Greg's body and pointing his gun at you.

Smoke wafts from its barrel.

You meet his cold eyes, and the gun in Cam's hand jumps with a blinding flame. You are pounded backwards into the ground. There is an echo of the blast. Pain is everything, and crimson fluid is everywhere. The world fades to black.

* * *

I don't regret the actions I have taken. The Movement, for all of its faults, has created some transparency of the mass corruption happening in world finance, and a better understanding of how it affects all of our lives. I hope I have given power back to the people once again and sincerely hope that they will not squander it. Though my obsession with Jeffrey Donahue has been personal, I hope you, the public, will understand that it is also universal. We are all toyed with by people like him. Without Jeffrey, I would have been an exec at some bank, working sixty hours a week and taking money from hardworking people for the silver-spoon community like him. His greed and contempt for the working class first led me into being an exploiter of the worst order, but then a savior to the people.

The violence that has happened is the result of Bloody Monday. They started it. Today I plan on finishing it, at least my beef with Jeffrey. It is me or him. If I don't make it, please keep my story and The Movement alive. And always watch those with money. They have a disease, and they will destroy others so that their own pile of ill-gotten gains will continue to grow. Stay strong. Stay skeptical. Stay vigilant.

Sincerely, Randall Waters (aka Jack Hamilton)

* * *

LIGHT SEEPS BACK into your eyes, and you realize you can't move your right arm. Breaths of air are excruciating. Cam shot you between the front of your shoulder and the vest at a downward angle. With your left arm, you reach for the backup pistol in your ankle holster, but Cam, the traitorous bastard, steps on your hand and kicks the gun free.

"Clear," Cam yells.

The cigar room door opens and Jeffrey walks out. He looks older, but still has the boyish, mischievous look, even with gray hairs and crow's feet. He is wearing a Kevlar vest under his Polo shirt and still has the air of a man owning the world. You cough up blood, feeling it building in your lungs. It's punctured.

"Is he going to die on me?" Jeffrey asks Cam. "Not before you get a shot off first, sir." Looking at Cam, you feel an odd moment of pride. Of course he betrayed you. He had all the characteristics that you had as a young man, which meant getting ahead by any means necessary. The younger you would have betrayed anybody to the next guy with more influence. What were you expecting? All you had to offer Cam was the elimination of powerful men and a life of hiding.

"Anything else I should know, Cameron?"

"Oren is out in the woods and should have been caught by now."

Jeffrey shakes his head. "Such a small, pathetic team. I'd be embarrassed to have such a group of worthless third-string players. But that's Randall for you, scraping the basement."

"Jack also left a diary behind," Cam says quickly.

Jeffrey's eyes light up. "Is that so?"

You try not to show hurt or outrage. Keep a stone poker face. Show nothing. Just don't let him know how important that memoir is. But something on your face betrays you, and Jeffrey catches it. He bends down, his blue eyes glowing to your dimming pair. His pupils are small, and the whites of his retinas are bloodshot. He's definitely cranked up on something.

"More flattering stories about me, huh?" You bite your lip and say nothing. He stands, his back to you. "I think you need to come clean and admit it, Randy." Jeffrey spins and points at you like he's in a video from the '80s. "You've got a crush on me."

He howls with laughter, and Cam chuckles.

"Where is this great piece of Shakespearian horseshit, Cammie-boy?"

"Out by the rose garden, sir. Buried in the front," Cam says.

You know you can't let Jeffrey find your memoir. If he does, he'll destroy it and The Movement. Everything you've built will be for nothing.

"I can't wait to read it . . . if I have insomnia. I'm sure it will put me to sleep like your other books did."

Jeffrey laughs again, and so does Cam. It's pathetic to see Cam in the slimy role of sycophant, but it's an opening.

"You're still not funny, Jeffrey," you manage to croak out. "Cam's just a toady. He'll sell you out to the next asshole."

"Is that so?"

"No, sir," Cam says, looking stern.

"Give me your gun. I want to finish this business myself," Jeffrey says with mischief brimming on his face. Cam steps off your hand and hands his pistol over. You flex your fingers, readying them for use.

"Safety off?"

"Yes, sir."

Boom! Smoke fills the room, and Cam falls to his knees, clutching his chest. His eyes are wide in disbelief as his face turns to an ashen, unnatural gray.

"You did your job very well, but you're too much like Randall. You can't be trusted."

It hurts to see him die like this, but you feel some satisfaction. A traitor, he'll burn in hell with everybody else, hopefully closer to the flames.

"Don't feel bad about that jerkoff dying," Jeffrey says. "Remember when that guy killed your little friend . . . what was his name. Otis? Oscar? That's it, Oscar. Cam let him through. Of course, the bullets were meant for you.

Cam should have let him keep shooting, but he felt it was a botched job and had to play fake hero. Oh well. We finally took you down." Jeffrey turns away with a gleeful smile.

With your free arm, you reach inside your jacket and find what you want. Fuck Jeffrey, Cam's corpse, and this world—you're ready to die.

"You know, Randy," Jeffrey says as he starts pacing. Here comes some convoluted self-aggrandizing speech put together months ago just for this occasion. "You and Cam are alike, poor trash thinking you can rise to my level by trying to impress people like me. Let me tell you why that's not possible."

See? So predictable. You're ready to finish this.

You pull the pin on the grenade with your thumb and hold the safety lever, ignoring the blowhard's speech, waiting for him to step closer. You focus on your life and the insanity of it all. You had ambitious dreams, dreams that didn't include other people, only you. What a waste. Maybe The Movement will continue after your death. The people will stand up, refusing to give their hard earned money to the wealthy. Maybe they will see the mistakes you made and still value The Movement, making it stronger.

Regardless, even if it is all a failure and things remain the same, at least your life will end in a blast.

You giggle, coughing up the blood you're drowning in, but you can't help yourself. Life is so absurd.

Jeffrey pauses and leans over you. The last words you ever hear are, "What's so fucking funny?"

Real-Time Retribution

THE OTHER PLAYERS quickly deserted the table. Wilbur had two aces, but Bull Jones had three, including two clubs. Wilbur called Bull a cheater.

"You gonna back up them words?" the gunslinger taunted.

Bull was the fastest draw in Kaiowa County. He also drank a ton of whiskey, but not enough for Wilbur to survive a shootout.

There was no exit.

Draw and die or walk and be branded a coward . . . which was worse than death.

Wilbur realized he could deal an ignoble fate.

So he drew and died, but not before squeezing his trigger and making Bull into a steer.

About the Stories

The Day We Shot Jesus on Main Street
Shotgun Honey, April 2012
An inspired train of thought about how megachurches are
opposite of Jesus's examples and how nothing, even a
blasphemous stunt, would get members to see this.

The Proxy
Thuglit #13, September/October 2014
Nominee, Macavity Award for Best Short Story
Thinking about the country's drug epidemic, the moral
issues involved, and how much somebody would sacrifice
for a family member.

Cop in a Well
Spinetingler Magazine, May 2016
Distinguished Mystery Story, *The Best American Mystery Stories of
2017*
Written with the idea of having a character escape an
impossible situation. After the story was rejected from the
Bouchercon anthology, *Murder Under the Oaks*, I changed the
location from North Carolina to Tennessee.

A Bro Code Violation
Spinetingler Magazine, August 2014
I hunted deer a few times in Oklahoma. What I remember
most is standing still and freezing.

Here's to Bad Decisions: Red's Longneck Hooch
Shotgun Honey, May 2015
I could hear an announcer dictating the downfall of a
character while selling his product. I had to write it.

Getting the Yes
King's River Life, September 2013
Written not long after I was engaged, it has nothing to do
with my wife and more about anxiety of the ring being good
enough.

Damn Good Dad
Flash Powder Burns, August 2012
A sad take on meth addiction and skewed priorities. I had heard stories about families suffering burns while trying to provide extra income.

Tim's Mother Lied
Shotgun Honey. January 2016
I sent the story to Shotgun Honey as a noir children's tale. They sent notes that it didn't work, so I rewrote the story straight from the child's point of view. It turned out better.

Maybelle's Last Stand
Shotgun Honey Presents Locked and Loaded, Both Barrels Volume 3, April 2015
Not sure of the origin, but I remember a vision of a blurry, menacing man sauntering up to a porch, not unlike *Once Upon a Time in the West.*

Because
Flash Fiction Offensive, May 2014
The working title was "The Boy Who Didn't Read." I saw the story from the middle first with the robbery and then broke down the reasons why it happened.

Incident on the 405
The Malfeasance Occasional: Girl Trouble, September 2013
Nominee, Anthony Award for Best Short Story
Nominee, Macavity Award for Best Short Story
I pictured two women from two different worlds colliding on Los Angeles's biggest parking lot.

Quack and Dwight
Jewish Noir, November 2015
Finalist, ScreenCraft Short Story Contest
Finalist, Derringer Award for Best Novelette
Nominee, Macavity Award for Best Short Story
Nominee, Anthony Award for Best Short Story
I worked on multiple drafts to get this story right and enlisted the aid of an LA County prosecutor and an expert in child services. Also, the editor, Kenneth Wishnia, called me out on putting too much starch in the Jewish meal.

Final Testimony
Flash Fiction Offensive, July 2017
Finalist, Derringer Award for Best Flash
Started out as a longer piece that got compressed into this story. I saw a desperate cop who sacrificed everything for a case, and it could be for nothing.

Not Sure Which Way I'm Headin'
All Due Respect Volume 4, September 2014
I'd wanted to write about the 1992 Los Angeles riots for quite a while. When I moved in LA in the late '90s, people talked about OJ and the riots all the time.

The Movement
Scoundrels: Tales of Greed, Murder and Financial Crimes, March 2012
I wanted to set the story with the Bohemian Club, but research proved to be difficult since it is a secretive society. So I opted for the nearby Russian River in an area where I used to work.

Real-Time Retribution
Flashshot, May 2011
I thought of a man in an impossible situation and how he might get out of it with some pride. A fun exercise in compression.

Acknowledgements

There are so many people I want to thank for helping make this collection possible. I'm afraid I'm missing several, but here are a few:

Gary Phillips, who gave me my first big break and opened several doors for me. Ron Earl Phillips, who I met at Bouchercon in St. Louis and told me about Shotgun Honey; since then I've had eight stories published with that outfit. Chris Rhatighan for being an early fan of my work and encouraging me send stories to All Due Respect. Eric Beetner for letting me read as unknown writer at Noir at the Bar LA. Kenneth Wishnia for inviting this goy to *Jewish Noir* and raising my profile. Todd Robinson, Tom Pitts, Jack Getze, Aldo Calcagno, Lorie Lewis Ham, Mike Monson, Claire Toohey, Rob Pierce, Hector Durate Jr., and Eric Campbell for accepting my stories and making them better. Holly West, Angel Luis Colón, Kelli Stanley, Hilary Davidson, Eryk Pruitt, Jordan Harper, S.W. Lauden, Kate Thornton, Kevin Barney, Sachin Mehta, Dylan Kohler, and Patricia L. Morin for your friendship and support. Everyone I've met in the great communities of Mystery Writers of America, Sisters in Crime, Bouchercon, and Left Coast Crime.

And AJ Hayes and William E. Wallace, whose absence is felt throughout the noir crime world. I miss both of you.

My biggest thank you goes to Stephen Buehler and Sarah M. Chen for the seven plus years of our (usually) weekly writing group. You've seen my prose at its roughest and helped make it better through hundreds of notes on countless drafts.

And, of course, Teresa: my editor, champion, and confidant. You've seen me at my best and my worst, and been a constant partner on this wobbly, uncertain journey of publishing and life. Lucky me.

About the Author

Travis Richardson has had over 40 short stories published, including finalists for the Anthony, Macavity, and Derringer Awards and a listing in *The Best American Mystery Stories*. A big supporter of short stories, he has reviewed all of Anton Chekhov's publicly available stories and attempted to read 1000 short stories in a year. Travis is the author of two novellas, *Lost in Clover* and *Keeping the Record*, and has also written and directed a handful of short films. He was raised in Oklahoma and currently lives in Los Angeles with his wife and daughter. Find out more at tsrichardson.com and chekhovshorts.com.

Made in the USA
Las Vegas, NV
22 April 2024

89015833R00114